Crossed Stars

ROSE PARKER JOHNSON

Crossed Stars

Chapter 1

The Meeting

AS ANNA ADAMOS traveled to her home's neighboring country, she felt like an explorer, hopeful for the treasures she might find. She admired the undeniable beauty as she drove away from her condominium in Prijipati City before dawn. Since Valtross was a country west of Namibia, the South Atlantic Ocean provided an elegant backdrop for the capital. She drove down the coast, appreciating the duality of untouched waters cresting against a slow slope on which her recent ancestors had built the city. The modern architecture of hard angles contrasted with the softness of the moonlit clouds floating within the deep-blue sky. The countless windows of the capital's black buildings twinkled in yellows and whites as the populous city awoke.

Sipping her large tumbler full of the coffee she had made for the long journey, she enjoyed the sights of her trip. All along the coast, Valtross was made up of more sprawling gray-and-black cities that sparkled as she drove south under the just-waking sky. Valtross's industrial development promised progress. And yet, all those qualities did not come close to awing Anna the way her country's neighbor of Stardade would.

After showing the patrol her passport, she crossed the border with ease. Trade and business travel between the countries was not only common but necessary. Stardade was an underdeveloped, gorgeous country west of Angola. Stardade let nature reign, for better or for worse.

As she continued to drive along the shore, the differences between the countries astounded her. The emerald-green mountains to the east weren't host to human habitation, amongst rolling hills within verdant valleys of trees, nestled the occasional log or brick cabin crafted of earlier times. Driving through a small logging town, she witnessed the blackened, caved-in roof of an abandoned, burned-down sawmill. Juxtaposed against the backdrop of this devastation rested a sleepy main street. Small establishments crafted of two-story wooden buildings were topped with what she could only assume were the owners' apartments. Well-versed in current events, Anna knew that part of the country's lack of development was due to the five-year-long civil war that ended only six months ago. The war's fire bombings had targeted companies and their assets, aiming to destroy industrialized areas.

When she approached the ferry docked on the mainland at a small line of rocky beaches, she considered how the landscape connected to recent history. The rebel left group—a zealous political party—was known as the Union for Mother Nature Party, also known as the Unimona Party. This party's ideals included allowing nature to reclaim the land that industries, especially mining companies, had ravished.

The extreme right—and ruling political party—was known as the National Stardade Workers' Party or Nasaw Party. This party fought in the name of progress, supposedly for progress's sake. But every educated person knew their number one priority was capitalism. The Nasaw Party wanted the country's continued laissez-faire—which meant the federal government would not interfere as the free-market economy ran its course. This economy's primary export, cobalt, was one Anna's country imported. To ensure continued international trade, the leaders of her own country of Valtross, an ally of the Nasaw Party, had provided aid during the war.

After the war claimed tens of thousands of victims, the Nasaw Party won. But at a high cost, perhaps higher than the leaders and their sympathizers had anticipated. Since then, the federal government had done its best to reclaim and rebuild the company land. However, with their national treasury depleted—and the country in a recession, heading for a depression—the restructuring process was slow.

Despite the ruling party's obvious win based on numbers, in some ways, the rebels had won. Anna could see how nature ruled the countryside of Stardade. And no matter how many warships and submarines had traversed this ocean before, the waters were quiet as she viewed them. She rolled her window down to smell the salty, fresh air.

From the cracked and pot-holed road, she drove onto the rickety dock as a surly man in overalls waved her forward. Following only two other cars, she drove onto the ferry. On the ship deck, an elderly man in a navy-blue captain's uniform smiled at her car, his laugh-lines creasing. He approached as she parked in the spot at which he pointed.

"I just love this electric-blue color," he said in a gruff voice, patting her side mirror. "This must be the deluxe version of the Adamos Rocket."

"Yes, it is," Anna said with a tight smile, hoping he didn't recognize her face.

"I own the Rocket in spring green. Just love all the Adamos Motor Group designs, really." He winked a fatherly gesture. "Great minds think alike."

"But fools seldom differ." She had said the follow-up to the saying without thinking.

The captain guffawed, and she joined in with a giggle, relieved she hadn't offended him.

"Very good, miss." He reached into the car and squeezed her shoulder, a foreign yet warm gesture to her. "Well, I must attend to my duties. Have a nice day."

Rolling up her window, she was relieved he had to leave. For the umpteenth time, she was glad people rarely knew her face. If he had recognized her, he probably would've talked endlessly about his love of the Adamos Motor Group. This line of conversation often came with countless questions for her.

Once en route to her destination of Stardade's island off the coast, she got out of her car. She had looked forward to enjoying the view since she had set the travel plans. She closed the door of her electric, luxury sedan manufactured by her family's company and headed to the upper deck of the ferry. Few people traveled with her at this hour, and she appreciated the peace her seldom solitude brought.

As the middle child of wealthy business owners, she was set to inherit the corporation along with her older brother and younger sister. Of course, she was proud of the conglomerate her parents had established in the name of greener energy. But she also wanted to build a name for herself on her own. Her passion was real estate, specifically municipal buildings, especially historical ones. She found that the older the building, the more charm, and stories it held.

But this international meeting she was traveling towards was a whole different ball of wax. On a business trip, she was on her way to meet with a potential client. If this meeting went well, her brokerage would represent Anna's family friend, Mark Rand, as he purchased the Wesley family land. This land would be profitable for Mark's mining company, the Rand Mining Corporation. Anna loved being a real estate broker and knew this sale could take her company to the next level. But this high-profile property opportunity had her in a tizzy.

Her parents had only added to the pressure. They were pushing her brokerage to obtain the property for Mark. They knew he would offer uninhibited access to the cobalt and other minerals common to the crust of the island's earth. This business move would promote the symbiotic relationship between the Rand and Adamos companies. Her parents used cobalt as a raw material to manufacture the batteries in their company's electric cars. And the limited resource was running out within the available Rand land. To complicate matters, Mark had insisted he remains anonymous as a party interested in the purchase.

While out here on the South Atlantic Ocean, though, Anna let the salty, cool breeze carry her worries away, at least for the time being. Business could wait until she arrived at her meeting. For now, she admired how the blue-green waters reflected the yellow sunlight as white sparkles, like an aquamarine gem. The wind picked up, tugging strands of her brunette hair from her bun and cooling her bare skin. Behind her, the waves crashed into the gray-and-blue coastal cliffs topped with vibrant grass. In front of her, in the distance, she saw luscious, green-and-gray mountains topped with white snow.

Too soon, the ferry docked on the sandy beach of Astiri Island. The single dock rested at the perimeter of the island's historic district. The district was known internationally for its quality mom-and-pop shops and diners. As much as Anna loved a good shopping spree, she didn't have time to enjoy walking the quaint streets of the strip mall. However, she did appreciate the endearing atmosphere of old-fashioned brick and ornamental iron-work as she drove over the cobblestone road out of town.

Anna drove west on a few miles of asphalt that made up the island's only highway. The road wound up to a southern cliff overlooking the stunning coast. Then, she followed her GPS north up the wet, dirt road toward her destination. The area must have just experienced rain, which she knew was frequent in this climate. This make-shift road wound through one of the island's drenched, vibrant forest valleys for ten miles.

She only passed one building on her drive through the forest. A classic, two-story brick hotel with maybe ten rooms sat tucked into a small clearing. The lamp-lit sign by the "road" displayed the name *Starlight Inn*. A small sign, hooked below its parent with a couple of chain links, claimed *Vacancy*. Anna made a mental note to check into this hotel later so she could rest for the evening before her journey home the next day. This trip had already been more tiring than she had anticipated, and the meeting hadn't even started yet.

The continued trek was slow-going due to the treacherous potholes full of mud. She prayed she wouldn't experience a mudslide. Though she knew mountains surrounded the landscape, she couldn't see them through the dense treescape. So that she wouldn't tempt fate, she shooed away the thought, *At least it isn't raining.*

To her immense relief, she pulled into a large, gravel driveway. She parked next to a red, classic Ford pickup truck. Based on the automobile's age, circa 1955, she knew the truck had to be gas-powered. Not to mention, importing the car, maintaining its functionality, and refurbishing its paint job must have cost a small fortune. She couldn't help but snub the supposedly energy-conscious, young Wesley for this purchase.

The driveway rested at the base of a grassy hill. From the hill's foot jutted a rectangular archway over a path up the hill. The rough, tree-branch archway was topped with a tasteful wooden sign that displayed the words *Wesley Estate*. As she gazed up at the sign, she noticed the words were wood burned into the sign. The carpentry and handwriting of the display had elegant eccentricities that only spoke of a handcrafted piece.

Looks like I'll be walking the rest of the way, she realized while examining the narrow trail. Feeling as bittersweet as the last dregs of her lukewarm coffee, Anna took one last sip to center herself. Before exiting her car, she looked in the sun-visor mirror. Her long, brown hair had started to escape its hair-sprayed cage in whisps. She did her best to recreate her bun without any hair products. Her chipmunk cheeks were a little flushed in anticipation of the meeting she was due to attend in fifteen minutes.

"You're gonna slay this meeting," she said to her brown eyes reflected in the mirror. "Go get 'em, tiger."

After letting out one more deep breath, she grabbed her black leather briefcase and stepped onto the driveway. The gravel crunched under her black, ballerina-style shoes. She couldn't help but peek into the Ford's windows to tut-tut at the lack of seatbelts. *This relic should be in a museum, not someone's only vehicle.* A crisp afternoon spring breeze teased up goosebumps on her bare skin, cooling her nerves. Glad she had decided to wear flats to complement her white blouse and black pencil skirt, she trudged up the steep hill's cobalt-and-rock cobblestone path to the log cabin. Not the first time in her thirty years she cursed her short legs. As much as she loved (slow) running, her body was not designed for climbing. With a small, trim frame, she was better suited for endurance running than incline hiking. Enduring this trek in tight business attire, briefcase in hand, was a struggle, but Anna was always up for a challenge.

She distracted herself by admiring the building she approached at a steady pace. Anna appreciated the elegance of the modest, efficient architecture constructed only of mahogany wood on a rectangular foundation. Smoke puffed from the home's chimney, indicating her client was home for their meeting. Although, considering the nice weather, she was surprised he had bothered with a fire. She noticed the sun's afternoon position off to the left as she hiked. The walking path arched to the northeast, trailing to the front of the house facing the west.

When Phillip Wesley—the sole surviving heir of the Wesley Mining Corporation—had suggested the two meet at his family home, she had found the request odd. *Why wouldn't we just meet at his office or a coffee shop?* she had wondered. But the decision had been his, and her goal was to keep this client happy and favorable to the Rand Mining Corporation's interests, which were also in favor of the Adamos Motor Group's interests.

Anna knocked on the evergreen-colored door before reminding herself to breathe. She was an excellent broker and had this deal in the bag.

Chapter 2

The Proposition

ANNA HADN'T ANTICIPATED just how stunning the young twenty-something would look when he opened the door. First, she noticed his eyes were as blue as the sky. Those eyes were as lively as a blue jay bird and stood out against his tan skin and black hair. Anna noticed the bags under his curious, tense gaze. At a height at least two heads above hers, his high cheekbones and dimples accented a forced smile. Five o'clock shadow darkened his face. He wore an outfit reminiscent of a lumberjack, complete with red-and-green plaid fleece, tattered jeans, and brown boots. His broad shoulders shifted forward towards her when he extended his hand.

"You must be Miss Adamos," he said in a deep, friendly voice. "I'm Phillip."

"Yes, nice to meet you." She mentally shook herself from her admiration as she shook his strong, warm hand. Based on the calluses she felt on his palm, she wondered if he worked with his hands. *Focus,* she thought. *This is a business meeting.*

"Come in." His tone was polite and formal, with a tinge of the same tension present in his eyes. He released her hand to gesture into his home. "Can I get you anything?

"I'm fine, thank you." She stepped over the threshold and followed him into the living room.

The space was set in an open floor plan below a staircase that zig-zagged up the front wall of the structure. The entire building was constructed of wood, save for the windows.

"Are you sure?" he asked. "I have coffee, water, tea …."

She heard his tired voice trail off as he watched her. For a moment, she forgot to respond as she took in the three-story-tall windows in front of her. The windows, just beyond the crackling fireplace to the left, made up the entire back wall of the house. The view overlooked a vast expanse of forest that led off to the breathtaking, white-capped mountain range to the southeast and the sparkling ocean to the northeast. The vista brought together a glorious, cloudless display of sky blue, snow white, granite gray, forest green, and ocean blue.

"Your reaction is surprising," he said next to her, "considering you're the wealthy heir to an industrial, automobile-based empire."

The comment startled Anna from her daze, making her turn to look into Phillip's fierce, blue eyes. In the sunlight from the windows, she realized his dark hair was brown, not black. A sardonic grin, coupled with a crinkled brow, tempered his handsomeness, making him look devilish. The man had done his homework.

"Interesting observation," she countered, "considering it comes from the wealthy heir to an industrial, mining-based corporation."

His barking laugh sounded sarcastic and accented the bitter taste in her mouth. "Of course, someone in your position would fail to understand the economics of Stardade." His eyes were blue fire, but his confident body language exuded an assured, righteous calm.

"Enlighten me." She wanted to cross her arms but didn't want to appear petulant, so she put a hand on her hip instead.

"Please, let's sit and talk." He gestured to the two brown vinyl armchairs facing the windows. He only sat once she did, then continued, "Stardade's entire economy suffers at the whim of Valtross."

"Oh, does it?" she challenged, crossing her legs and placing her hands on her top knee. "Last I checked, your federal government has only benefited from its relationship with Valtross."

"Your country leeches off our land's vein of minerals to obtain your *precious cobalt.*" He spat the last two words as he leaned forward in his chair. "Those in power seek only to benefit themselves, the majority of the population be damned."

"You're saying Stardade's economy doesn't benefit from the lucrative export of cobalt?" she asked rhetorically while giving into the urge to cross her arms.

"How can we count our benefits against so many struggles brought on by *your* import?"

"Such as?"

"Where to begin?" He sounded exasperated. As he spoke the list, he counted the reasons on his fingers. "The child labor common to the third-party companies that your country's corporations hire. The environmental devastation those companies inflict on our mainland, especially our small island. Those effects have spread farther than you could ever imagine."

When he paused, she resigned herself and promoted, "Go on. I need to hear your piece."

"In fact, Valtross has turned a blind eye to the environmental effects that affect its own land, too." He closed his counting fingers into a fist, then prodded the armrest of his chair with his index finger. "There are inherent safety risks in the process of mining *and* extraction. Not to mention, corruption runs rampant in every single step of the ordeal." He reclosed his fist and pounded the armrest as though resting his case.

She paused, absorbing these numerous issues of which she knew little. Though she knew well of the international trade, of course, she didn't know much about these supposed far-reaching effects. Naturally, the process of mining cobalt and manufacturing cars took miners and workers, so production took a toll. But she had grown up hearing the benefits of electric cars for people and the environment, which she had always thought far outweighed the cost. *Why haven't I heard my parents discuss these problems?* she wondered. *Have I turned a blind eye to the environment and people's issues, or have they?*

"You didn't even know," he said, sitting back and looking satisfied, "did you?"

His attitude sparked the flames of her next words. "Like you don't stand to gain from the industry. You own all this land." She gave a sweeping gesture towards the window.

"My parents owned this land. When they died, along with all my brothers, during our civil war—which you must know was brought on entirely by *your* country—I inherited the property."

She paused again, this time to process the hurt in his words. His eyes showcased his blues with unfiltered grief. Though he wasn't crying, Anna felt certain he might if they continued this line of discussion. His passionate sorrow wafted in billows from his entire being.

Of course, she knew the facts of the two country's shared politics and the details that had led to the five-year war still fresh in both of their memories. However, the news outlets of Valtross undoubtedly skewed the presentation of these facts. *I thought Stardade caused its own war.* While she wasn't aware of any nationalized propaganda machine in place, she was aware enough of how the world worked to credit the possibility. She did know her country was considered, throughout the world, as an obnoxious, entitled bully. Too proud to ask clarifying questions about her thoughts, she filed them away for later consideration.

Sure, she, too, had done her homework and known of Phillip's familial loss. This background wasn't difficult to obtain when his family's tragic situation had been plastered all over the headlines in Valtross. His story wasn't surprising, counted amongst the tens of thousands of war-related deaths. Phillip's situation was unique to the truth that his influential, wealthy family name stood to change the economic landscape of Stardade. His purchasing and selling power—now levied by only one man— could turn the tide of the entire country's welfare. But he didn't seem eager to allow this capitalist industrialization. *Even though his parents died for the Nasaw Party cause, maybe he has grown bitter towards the party. Maybe he is a Unimona Party sympathizer.*

In the presence of the sole survivor of this tragedy, the topic heavy in the air, Anna's chest tightened. The frustration that had gusted the wind in her sails slowed to a breeze, then died altogether.

"And the decision concerning the land's sale falls to you alone," she said, lowering her voice and letting her tone soften.

His body language eased up the smallest amount as she tempered her approach. Phillip nodded, eyes falling to the modest, antique coffee table between them. He seemed to acknowledge that her vibe had shifted to compassionate sympathy.

"So," she said. "Why agree to this meeting at all?"

"I need to consider all my options now that Stardade has entered a recession." His eyes still examined the table.

"Brought on by the war," she said, expressing her growing understanding of his perspective.

He nodded again, looking into her eyes. His expression contained an ocean of despair sparkling with a hint of hope.

"Let's discuss your options," she said, pulling her laptop from her briefcase.

Chapter 3

The Appeal

EXAMINING THE PRESENTATION on Anna's computer screen, the two discussed the property's potential. Once she had shifted her defensive stance, instead choosing to listen to his side and present real-estate facts, Phillip followed her lead. He talked at length, seeming to understand she was there to hear him out and help his estate's endeavors. But he never let his guard down, never revealing whether he was leaning towards selling the land.

As much as the process pained Anna, she listened to all her client had to say about his side. At length, they discussed the bleak politics surrounding their border-sharing countries. She had underestimated just how broken her country's outlook on their neighbor was.

With the aid of her compassionate diplomacy, the meeting proceeded professionally and calmly. They discussed well into the evening, long after the sun descended on the front west side of the house. The colors of the windows' view darkened and deepened into midnight blues and purples. The sky overhead twinkled with hundreds more stars than Anna was used to seeing above her home's cityscape.

Anna glanced at her watch and jumped out of her chair when she saw the time was after nine.

"What's wrong?" Phillip asked, his eyebrows raising.

"Time got away from me," she said, hesitating to pack up her laptop as she examined the stubble on his chin.

She didn't want to rush the conclusion of their discussion, especially considering she had a pang of sadness at the thought of leaving. This thought surprised her at first. Despite their initial hostility, the two had established a tentative truce in the name of business. She still felt frustrated by the blunt way he expressed his favorability for his country while discounting the qualities of her home country. More than once, her blood had boiled during his explanations that he expressed as facts rather than the opinions they were.

However, she had done her best to allow him the space he needed to speak without stamping down his views. To purchase the property for Rand, she knew she had to keep this client as agreeable as possible. Only by listening could she establish the best approach to the sale. And this process would obviously take some careful attention and persuasion. In the meantime, she had the unique opportunity to make a connection with a Stardade citizen and learn more about a country with which her family did considerable business. Setting her own frustration aside, his perspective fascinated her. Somehow, this man managed to sound both arrogant and humble. He was proud of his country, a land rich in resources but not money.

"Do you have somewhere you have to be?" he asked, rising from his chair.

"No, I just didn't mean to keep you so late." She was trying to keep the situation formal, even though the hour had dripped well past business hours. "I apologize."

"No need to apologize." His tone also sounded formal as he put his hands in his pockets. "We had more to discuss than I think either of us realized."

"Would you like to set up an additional meeting soon?" She thought she had managed to refrain from sounding hopeful, but she couldn't be certain.

"Yes, if it's convenient, we ought to. I need to sleep on this decision." Looking out over the darkened land, he appeared sheepish for the first time in her presence. "This land meant everything to my family. Our—*my*—property is all I have left of them. This choice is the most important decision I might ever make."

"I understand." She nodded, then closed her laptop and placed the device in her briefcase.

"Where are you staying, the Starlight Inn?" He walked her to the door after she clicked the briefcase shut.

"I haven't booked a room yet."

"Oh no." He halted, causing her to turn towards him.

"What's wrong?"

"If you didn't get a reservation and key, you're out of luck. The couple that runs the bed and breakfast goes to bed at eight."

"Don't they have someone running the counter?"

"Not in this area. Everyone stays put once the sun goes down, so the owners just take calls for immediate needs."

"But I have an immediate—never mind, I'll find another hotel in town."

"Bad news. The road through the valley is too dangerous to drive at night."

"How's that?"

"Take your pick. No streetlights. Blind turns. Countless wildlife that wanders into the street."

She sighed, losing her patience. "What do you propose I do?"

"Stay here."

"At your house?"

"Of course." His host-worthy grin made her pause.

"I can't do that," she said when she collected her thoughts.

"Why not? I have four bedrooms."

"You're a client."

"A client that would feel guilty for the rest of his life if you died on his private road." He didn't quite pout, but his eyes quivered with his plea.

She sighed, louder this time, then considered her options. After a brief pause in which she almost forgot herself in his eyes, she said, "If you insist."

"I do." Eyes dancing, he grinned. His face was the picture of victory, with his dimples accenting his straight, white teeth. "This way to the guest suite."

Following him up the wooden staircase, she rolled her eyes.

The second floor housed the quaint yet accommodating suite with three bedrooms and two bathrooms.

"You can sleep in any of these rooms. There are fresh sheets and towels on each bed. Hotel-size toiletries in the bathrooms, too."

"Expecting company?"

"I'm playing around with the idea of offering short-term rentals. I need to diversify my income streams, and tourism is lucrative here."

"This house would attract guests with that view alone." She tipped her head towards the large windows still visible from the landing.

"My thoughts, exactly. Oh, and there are even some spare clothes of my brothers you can wear if you'd like. I left some in the dressers in case guests would need them."

She looked from darkened doorway to darkened doorway.

"Of course," he added, "they're clean clothes."

"These were their rooms?" The question tumbled out of her mouth before she could stop herself.

He nodded. "That one was mine." He pointed to the one on the far left. "That one was Matthew's." He indicated the one in the middle. "That one was Ethan's." He ended at the one on the far right.

"My duffel is in my car, so I think I'll just—"

"Please, don't go outside."

She raised her eyebrows as a question.

"Bears."

"Ah."

"The master bedroom is just above you," he pointed to the ceiling, "so just knock on the ceiling if you need anything."

A charmed giggle escaped her lips. "I think I'll just text if I run into any issues, but I should have everything I need."

"Well, then, goodnight, Miss Adamos."

"Goodnight, Mr. Wesley."

He started to walk away.

"Mr. Wesley?" She watched him turn back towards her. "Thank you."

Chapter 4

The Rescue

SOMETIME AFTER MIDNIGHT, Anna realized she would probably spend most of the night with her mind racing too fast for her to be able to doze off. She tossed from one side of the bed to the other, trying not to think about the fact that she was trying to sleep in a dead man's bed. Though that was the least of her worries, the thought was one of the many that zoomed through her mind. Too bothered by the idea of sleeping in a client's childhood bed, she had shut herself inside the middle bedroom.

In the dark room, she watched the dust that floated through the shafts of soft starlight and moonlight. The celestial lights drifted through a crack in the curtains. Her eyes roved to the unreal amount of stars visible from her vantage point. She could even see the full moon peeking its pale face into the top corner of the frame. When she shifted down in the bed, she could see the entire glory of the moon. She wished she was a celestenaut (the Valtross equivalent of an astronaut), exploring that desolate, crevassed moonscape. On the moon, she could build the most beautiful architecture without interfering with any living creatures. At this moment, she didn't want to be the wealthy heiress of a politically motivated corporation.

She was hung up on her parent's involvement in the supposed corruption of her national government. During these quiet hours of introspection, she was embarrassed at how ill-prepared she had been to defend her country and corporation's interlinked actions. Worse than that, for some reason, she could not fathom. She was upset she had disappointed Phillip. Before she had even met him, she had disappointed him.

The sound of a fire alarm startled Anna from her thoughts. She launched from the bed and flew from the bedroom onto the stairs' landing. When she registered that the alarm came from below, she descended the stairs two at a time. At the bottom of the stairs, she paused to listen again and determined the sound came from another room.

Anna hustled to the left, through the archway into the kitchen, to find the room full of smoke. She coughed as she ducked below the billowing, black smoke. As she made her way deeper into the kitchen, she saw flames licking up the top cabinets from an appliance on the counter. The toaster oven was on fire. Phillip's tall form stood off to the side, fiddling with a fire extinguisher as he coughed.

"Give it here!" she demanded around coughs.

She grabbed the extinguisher and pulled its pin before spraying white foam on the toaster. The fire was out in seconds, but smoke still wafted in the room.

"Open the windows," she coughed, pulling a dish towel from the countertop.

Phillip was coughing as he attempted to shove open the window over the sink. Anna waved the towel in the direction of the smoke detector on the ceiling. When the alarm wouldn't stop, she ditched the towel to help him open the window. She was so short that she had to climb on top of the counter. From that position, she could see that he was trying to open a locked window. She flipped the locks, and Phillip easily pushed the window up.

"Just sit on the floor," she said, still coughing as she jumped down.

Mercifully, he followed her instructions. Well, sort of, because he lay down on his back.

The alarm continued warning of danger. Anna grabbed the towel from where she had thrown it on the floor. Her hand wrapped in the towel, she yanked the toaster's plug from the wall. Blue-white electricity sparked from the socket to the plug, but only a small shock. She was glad the spark hadn't hit her skin. Even in that crazed moment, she was proud that she hadn't squealed at the startling flash of light.

Next, she unlocked and opened the side door, then resumed waving the towel toward the detector. Finally, the alarm stopped blaring, so she collapsed on the floor next to Phillip. Though the smoke still thickened the air in the room, it was dissipating, turning less black and more gray.

"What happened?" she asked, chest heaving with coughs as they lay next to one another.

He shrugged, coughs still coming but slower. His white undershirt was tight across his pec muscles above his loose, plaid pants. "I was makin' toast. Guess I left it in too long. Might've forgotten." He lethargically shifted his gaze from the ceiling to Anna. His pupils were dilated so much that the blue was only a thin rim.

"Are you drunk?" she asked.

He nodded, dropping his eyes to her long, loose hair splayed on the floor between them.

Her cheeks grew warm as she felt a pang of embarrassment under his gaze. She realized she was only wearing the white, lacey slip she had on under her business clothes yesterday. Hopefully, she hadn't experienced a wardrobe malfunction when she had bounded and climbed around his kitchen like a monkey.

"Your hair is longer than I thought it was," he whispered in a hoarse voice.

When he reached for a lock of her hair, she sat up out of his reach. Though she couldn't help but feel excited about him playing with her hair as she gazed into those blue eyes, she knew they needed to remove themselves from the situation. Her client was drunk, and the gesture was born of lowered inhibitions.

"Come on," she said, standing. She crouched to pull on his warm, dense bicep.

"Huh?"

"Let's get you to bed."

"But my toast," he said, shaking his arm free from her grasp and coughing.

"Your toast ... is toast." She punctuated her comment with a cough.

Phillip's coughing laugh started slowly, then erupted into giggles. These giggles were so strong they wracked his whole body, making him roll around on the polished wood floor. He held his belly as he cracked up.

Watching this spectacle, Anna began laughing, too. She bent over with the force of her giggles. The two shared the laughter, causing a feedback loop that lasted several minutes. Their laughter sounded husky with smoke damage. They wound down with a shared, content sigh.

"Ready for bed?" she asked in a strained voice, wiping away her tears.

She held out her hand, which he took. After some maneuvering, he was on his feet and stumbling to the stairs with her arm around his toned waist. Eventually, after trudging up all three flights together, she helped him plop into bed.

"I owe you," he said with a gravelly voice.

"It wasn't that big of a deal." She put her hands on her hips. "You would've handled the fire just as soon as you pulled the pin on that fire extinguisher."

"Where'd you learn to do that?"

"I was a camp counselor. Training included a mandatory fire extinguisher discharge."

"How can I ever repay you for saving my life?"

"Buy me a coffee tomorrow," she suggested, just wanting to go to bed as she walked away, "and we'll call it even."

"Miss Adamos?"

At the threshold, she turned back to face him. "Please, at this point, we're on a first-name basis."

"Thank you, Anna."

"Goodnight, Phillip."

Chapter 5

The Encounter

SLEEPLESS NIGHTS WERE no stranger to Phillip, but they certainly weren't getting any easier. This morning, he had woken up with a headache followed by embarrassing memories of nearly burning down his family home. He leaned the small of his back against the kitchen counter and watched the dawning sunlight stretching lazily along the hardwood floors. He regarded his blackened toaster apologetically and spared a thought for how last night could have gone very differently. He had half-expected little Miss Adamos to make a play for the sale when he had offered her a reward for putting out the fire.

He still wasn't sure what to make of Anna. She had come in as the picture of business, tight bun and monochromatic clothes. He had fully anticipated he would despise her as the epitome of the greedy, heartless capitalists running wild in Valtross. He hadn't anticipated her facade dropping as soon as she saw the view of the Sidras Mountains sprawling across the horizon. The moment had made her seem human enough that Phillip had shared more than he'd ever intended about his dislike of her homeland. Again, Anna had surprised him.

She had listened. She hadn't just been feigning interest to suck up to him either; she had debated him earnestly but compassionately. Perhaps there were some rare, decent Valtrossians.

Faint footsteps sounded on the stairs, and Phillip looked up to see Anna descending. She didn't appear to see him at all. As she walked down, her eyes were fixed on the sun rising over the Sidras, her face soft with awe. Her hair cascaded down her back, swishing with each step-down. As he watched, he noticed she had tied back the top portion of her hair in a ponytail that swung down the rest of her loose hair. The dawn cast her in gold, painting her white blouse and lighting her frizzles, which had come loose from the half-ponytail, into a halo. She was too pretty to look at and too beautiful to look away from.

"Morning," Phillip rasped when she reached the bottom of the stairs.

Anna startled and turned.

He gave her a little wave, then called from the kitchen, "Good to see you survived the night."

She crossed her arms. "I could say the same."

He nodded in concession. "Touché."

Anna gave the mountain sunrise one last lingering look before coming to join Phillip in the kitchen. "Thank you for your hospitality."

"Thank you for your heroism."

"Sure," she said dryly. "Anything for a client."

He shifted his weight off the counter. "About that."

She looked up sharply. "What?"

Phillip met her gaze evenly. "I can't give up my family's land."

Her mouth pinched slightly. "Oh."

"I considered it, but Anna … I can't."

"All right," she said.

"I'm sorry."

"No, don't be. It's—" She tucked some wayward strands behind her ears and squared her shoulders. "It's fine. But I believe you still owe me a coffee?"

He nodded and offered a smile. "I do."

"Maybe we could discuss your latest thoughts?"

"We certainly could," he said. "But I won't be changing my mind."

She hummed in polite disagreement.

⎯⎯⎯

The two took separate cars into town so that Anna's vehicle would be closer to the ferry dock. Her plan was to go back to her home country after their final meeting. As he turned the key in the ignition, he felt an odd sensation in his chest. He considered the fact that he might never see her again after coffee. His mixed feelings resonated with both relief and regret. He needed the real estate agent to leave him and his land alone, but he didn't want her to leave his life. Maybe these emotions were coming from gratefulness for her saving his life and home last night.

She followed his gas-powered truck off the gravel and down the dirt road. *She probably wonders why I drive this kind of vehicle,* he mused. *I'll have to explain to her the benefits of staying classic.* He patted the steering wheel lovingly. *Old Bessie deserves her road time.*

As he drove through the forest, he did his best to go slow and indicate his turns well ahead of time. He could have left her in the dust but had decided instead to be a good Samaritan. He wasn't sure why. He had grown fond of the corporate princess.

Plus, driving slowly afforded him the opportunity to take in the valley that he had adored his entire life. Glancing in the rearview mirror, he felt certain Anna appreciated the hints of the ocean and mountain views peeking through the greenery. Perhaps his plan for the good of his home, island, and country was working. He had chosen his house as their meeting spot because he knew the locale would showcase the gorgeous environment.

Though he had calculated his decision for their meeting, his invitation for her to stay over had been spontaneous. There was some bewitching quality about Anna that made him want more time with her. And he had wanted to protect her, too, when she had planned to traverse the valley by night. By all accounts, he should have left her to the bears. She wanted to buy his land for some anonymous client, one that undoubtedly intended to industrialize the untouched landscape.

Yet, he sensed a good heart in her. While their introduction had gotten off to a rocky start, she had seemed willing to learn. He might not know her upbringing nor the lies she was fed as a child. But he was starting to realize it might have been too harsh of him to judge an heiress based on her parent's sins even if she did drive one of their cars and express knowledge of the "benefits" of electric.

All this cognitive dissonance rattling in his brain about Miss Adamos and the future of his land had led him to muse late into last night, whiskey in hand. As he had mulled over the meaning of it all, he had lost track of how many drinks he'd had. When he stood to go to bed, he realized he needed to get some food in his stomach. He must have bungled the toaster setting when he put his bread in. Then, his musings distracted him once again as he went back to his drink in the living room. Thus, the great toaster incident. He waved the embarrassment from his mind, gracious that Anna was still willing to spend time having coffee with the fool who drunkenly set his own house on fire.

He parked in the lot outside the café in the historic district. He realized he had parked next to the unmistakable, hot-pink Corvette of his childhood friend, Jaqueline Fox. Unfortunately, he had taken the last spot in the row, so Anna had to drive to another section of the parking lot.

When he exited the car, Jaqueline walked up at the same time, coffee in hand, to her own car. Her ginger hair was pulled into a ponytail, her freckles sporting the fresh sheen of her recent morning run.

"Philly," she said, an ear-to-ear smile on her face, "fancy meeting you here."

"Yeah," he said, distracted as he made sure Anna parked okay. He only realized later just how grumpy his next words sounded. "Odd when we live in a small town with one coffee shop."

"What's with you?" she asked, opening her car door.

"Sorry. I'm heading into a business meeting. Talk later?"

"Text me." Clearly miffed, she got into her car and sped off.

Jaqueline is a good friend, he reminded himself as he walked up to Anna. *Take the time to text her later and explain everything.*

The two walked into the shop together. To her credit, Anna didn't press him on the land sale until they were both tucked into a bistro table at Café Sterna with steaming mugs of black coffee. He was surprised that she liked her coffee the same way he did.

"So," she asked, "what changed?"

"Everything." He leaned forwards into the aromatic steam rising from his coffee. "And I *won't* give up the last thing I have."

"If the payout is an issue—"

"It's not about the money," he interrupted. "It's about family land. You might not understand. You grew up with your wealth."

"You'd hold it against me?" she asked.

"No, but I'd rather be without money than without my home."

"You could get a new home, even grander than your current one."

"I don't need a grander home. I like the one I have."

"Then, you could get a similar one. There are plenty of places with comparable views."

He scoffed. *Is she really attempting to deny how the mountain-seaside view had arrested her every time she caught a glimpse?* The claim was laughable. "Oh, really? Name three in Stardade."

"Well, I haven't seen much of Stardade," she said.

"What all have you seen outside of Valtross?"

"A decent amount." She leaned in closer, the knuckles of her hands inching a hair's breadth from his. Her eyes were bright with enthusiasm. As she spoke, he didn't move his hands. "I've been through all of Scandinavia. I studied Scandinavian architecture while at university, but the blueprints and photos can't begin to compare with seeing the buildings in person. I admire efficient designs, and you don't see much more efficiency than eco-designs. It's all about maximizing space with limited materials. Some architects find it too limiting, but I like the challenge."

"So, that's why you went with your family's real-estate business instead of the electric cars."

Anna pulled back and crossed her legs. "That's why I *founded* Adamos Realty," she corrected icily.

Founded? That was ... that was rather impressive. Phillip had looked into the company when Anna had first reached out to him. Adamos Realty (AR) had been around for six years, starting right before the war broke out. The company had somehow pulled out of the red every year. In light of the fact that the war was completely over, it only made sense that the realtors would expand outside of Valtross.

But for Anna to have not only started the company but kept it afloat during those first rocky years ... it was frankly impressive. She must have started AR when she was twenty-four years old. Phillip, at that exact age, couldn't begin to imagine starting a company this year. Even with help from the property sale money, it would be a massive undertaking.

He clasped his hands around his mug and slouched fully onto the table. She was looking closed off again, the same as when he'd first opened the door and let her into his home. Their rapport had dissolved. Although he didn't imagine that he would ever see her again after they finished their coffee, he would have liked for their acquaintanceship to end on better terms than it had started.

"That's truly impressive," he offered.

Anna smiled faintly into her mug. "Kind of you to say."

"Did you ever have doubts that you could pull it off?" he asked, trying to salvage the conversation by prompting her to share more.

"No. Housing is a need, and I knew I could help meet it. My first clients were local people who knew and valued my name beyond my family. My next challenge is building in an international market."

She leaned forward onto the table, and her knuckles brushed against the back of his hand. An involuntary tremor passed over his hand, and he clutched his mug tighter to stop it. She pulled her mug closer to her body, but she was still leaning in. There was a glint in her eye that let him know exactly what her thoughts were.

"The Wesley Estate is not for sale," he said firmly.

"You keep saying that," she huffed.

"And I will continue saying that until the end of time. You can't buy it."

"First of all, I'm legally required to tell you that Adamos Realty will not be purchasing the land for development."

He raised his eyebrows.

"An anonymous investor is interested in your estate. That being said, this wealthy entity could make you a very wealthy man, Phillip."

"Hmm, in that case—still no."

"I haven't heard a credible reason as to why."

"I told you last night that my family died during the civil war. My parents could have sold the property a dozen times over, but they never did. My land is worth more than its profits. I can't sell my homestead. It's the last piece left of my family."

"Hmm," Anna said. "I suppose I can respect that."

With the worst timing imaginable, a graying, older man pressed in from behind Anna and deposited a croissant at her elbow. "If memory serves," he said smarmily, "you have a weakness for sweets."

Phillip tossed an incredulous look from the invading man to Anna's nearly empty mug of black coffee.

Anna looked up and over her shoulder, and her face lit with recognition as she sprang to her feet. "Mark!"

As she dove into his arms, Phillip looked Mark over with a critical eye. He wore a full silk suit—entirely out of place in the homely environment of the modest café. On his feet, he had adorned impractical, pointed-toed cowboy boot monstrosities with panels of snakeskin and cobalt-studded spurs. His entire attire had no purpose in the valley. Still hugging Anna, Mark turned his head over her shoulder and made direct eye contact with Phillip.

His soulless eyes looked beady and black. Anna released her hold, but Mark didn't release her. Phillip briefly considered cutting in, but then Anna turned out of Mark's arms, and he finally let her go.

"Phillip," Anna said, a smile quirking her lips as she faced him again, "this is a close family friend, Mark. Mark, this is Phillip. He lives at one of the properties my company is trying to acquire."

Before Phillip could stand, Mark, stepped so close to his seat that he couldn't stand without moving the table. From above, Mark seized his hand and executed a cold, textbook handshake with a crocodile grin.

"Ah, I see!" He looked down his nose at Phillip, leaving the distinct impression that he had judged the younger man and found him insignificant. Mark let go of Phillip's hand and turned back to his supposed friend to say, "I was wondering what brought you here!"

"My first time in Stardade," Anna said. "But what about you? What brings you here?"

Mark stepped away, and Phillip began to relax gradually. "Business, I'm afraid. No sight-seeing tours for me."

Though he would rather not, Phillip moved to pull out a chair for Mark for the sake of etiquette. But Anna waved him back with a small smile. "Philip has been kind enough to allow me to sample the local cuisine as we chatted."

"How kind of him," Mark said, stepping back into Phillip's space to claw his shoulder. "Although it seems he neglected to mention the best part. Café Sterna makes the best chocolate croissants on the island. They're baked in-house if memory serves." He really was something, a Valtrossian trying to play tour guide in Stardade.

"They're actually made by one of the Astiri residents, Granny Hamal," Phillip said, "and she brings them each morning. But they are the best around."

Mark made a neutral sound in the back of his throat.

"Philip and I were discussing my travels and the different kinds of real estate deals I've helped broker," Anna said. Her body was turning back to Phillip, and she nodded at Mark in a clearly telegraphed farewell.

Not clear enough, apparently.

"Of course," Mark said knowingly. "Ah, have you told him about the deals you observed in Morocco?"

The effect the words had on Anna was immediate. Her smile dimmed until it was nearly a scowl, and her eyebrows crinkled together at the top of her nose. If Mark was a family friend, it might have been difficult for her to send him off. It might not be any better for Phillip to send him off either, though. He didn't know their dynamic. After all, he'd only met Anna yesterday.

"It hadn't come up …" Anna demurred.

They were fortuitously saved from prolonged, forced interactions with the socially oblivious businessman when his phone began to ring a standardized ringtone. Mark promptly withdrew his phone, stared at the caller ID, and sighed with unnecessary woe.

"My apologies," he said to Anna, completely ignoring Phillip, which suited him perfectly fine. Phillip knew he wasn't quite able to contain the relief from his expression. Mark continued, "I'm afraid I'm needed."

After a brief pause, during which Anna nodded encouragingly, Mark clomped his way back across the café with his ridiculous, pristine suit and offensively gauche boots. With a strong sense of good riddance, Phillip watched Mark slide through the door. He reached blindly for his mug to finish off his first morning dose of caffeine.

He was entirely unprepared to look back at Anna and find her grinning back at him with satisfaction.

"Oh!" Anna gasped, just a second too late, as Phillip fumbled his mug and spilled coffee over his lap. "I'll get napkins!"

"No," Phillip said, standing abruptly and banging his knee hard into the table leg. He saw Anna's coffee mug jump but without tumbling. He winced as he managed to stand. "I'll be right back."

The coffee was no longer scalding, so no serious damage had been done other than the total devastation of his dignity. He made straight for the restrooms and grabbed a handful of paper towels to begin blotting his pants dry. His jeans were so dark in this lighting that it was hard to tell if he was getting the stain out. He strained his eyes at his pants legs. *Maybe no one else will be able to see the stain once it dries,* he sighed. *But what if they can?*

He'd really prefer not to return to Anna, who managed to look put together despite the crumpled collar of her blouse and loose hairs evading the tied-back portion of her hair. Meanwhile, he had a stain that made it look like he hadn't managed to get to the bathroom in time. Phillip drew closer to the bathroom window to use the sunlight. He was just canting his hips to try to get the best lighting when a memorably smarmy voice drifted in.

"… our schematics for the mine place the slag heaps close to the island's historic district, but Stardade's laws are clear in our rights to place the waste anywhere we deem appropriate on our legal property, environmental impacts not-withstanding …."

Phillip's hands clenched into fists, scrunching up his paper towels. Realization hit him as a splash of piping-hot rage. *Mark is the unnamed investor that Anna works for.* Astiri was the only island of Stardade, and there was only one property bordering the historic district: the Wesley Estate. Not to mention, only one person had approached Phillip for purchasing so far.

He snarled and chucked his paper towels in the bin. He'd been such an idiot to think that Anna had been sincere with her bright, brown eyes and earnest words. No wonder she had wanted Mark to back off at the table: she hadn't secured the Wesley land for him yet. He'd probably been checking in to confirm that Anna had gotten the purchase.

"That location is the most cost-effective and efficient," Mark's irritating voice continued from outside, "and moving in a different direction will slow us down and waste more money. We keep the plans as they are. If the community is really *that* concerned, we can donate to a local museum or something to win back favor."

The fact that Anna was planning on conniving his property away under false pretenses was already infuriating enough. But worse yet, Anna and Mark were scheming to knowingly destroy the historic district. *That overbearing, two-faced, geriatric skin tag of a dead opossum!* He had not five minutes ago been waxing lyrical about Granny Hamal's chocolate croissants, feigning interest in the nuances of Astiri's culture. *The wretched audacity!*

Betrayal burned through Phillip's body as he stormed back into the bistro area of the café. He went back to their table, but he could not bring himself to sit back down across from that round-faced Jezebel.

"Phillip?" Anna said gently. "Everything all right? Do you need ice, or—"

"You know—" Phillip spat. "You know what the funny thing is? I actually *believed* you. I bought into your lie. I should have known that there's no such thing as a Valtrossian with morals."

Anna blinked, and her smile drooped to a more neutral expression. "What on earth are you talking about?"

"You!" he snarled. "You and Mark, *plotting* how you could get your hands on my land so you could just *raze* it."

"I … What? I wouldn't—"

"It's up! It's over! Unless you know about *another* Stardade island with *another* estate bordering a historic district that's big enough to house a slag heap."

"But you're not accepting the offer."

"And if I had?" he demanded. "You'd have kept mum about the part where Mark's going to throw all the waste next to the historic district? What wouldn't you and your family stoop to in order to get more money?"

"Mark wouldn't." She actually looked shocked, which only made Phillip angrier. "You must have misunderstood."

"What wouldn't he do? What wouldn't any of you do?"

"Okay, look," she said. "I don't know who that 'any of you' is in reference to, but you're blowing this way out of proportion. You're judging the situation before you know it. Mark knows that I'm passionate about incorporating the environment into my designs. He listened to me talk about it enough times in college." She must have had the habit of talking too much when she was nervous because she was still going. "He knows how much I care about the environment. He would never hide intentions like *this* for the sake of some business deal."

For a moment, Phillip was speechless with rage. Even confronted with her sins, Anna was content to keep on her sweet, nostalgic, story-telling denial. He glared, clench-jawed, at her as she stared innocently back at him.

"I'll talk to Mark," she said, gesturing to the chair across from her. "Sit down, and I'll call him now. We'll figure it out together."

"Doesn't matter." He roughly shoved his chair back under the table. "I don't need excuses or cover-ups. I'm not selling, and you can take your *electric* car right on back to the ferry and onto the mainland. We're through." He had said *electric* like the word was a curse.

"I'll call him," she said. "I'll let you know what I find out."

His mouth twisted in a pained, furious grimace. "Don't bother."

Anna followed him out of the café and back to the parking lot, but she didn't try to stop him from climbing in his truck and driving off. He couldn't tell if he was more relieved or disappointed.

He'd shown her his home, shared his anecdotes, and bared his strangling, desperate rage about the conditions of his country and his family. Anna had seen it all. Yet, in her calculations, the cobalt mines were worth more than all else. He should never have gotten mixed up with Valtrossians. This meeting had always been doomed to end with failure.

Chapter 6

The Boy

MARK WASN'T A man who often frequented coffee shops. He was the kind of man who made his way quickly and efficiently to the office and sent someone whose time was less valuable to get his coffee for him. But he'd woken up slightly earlier than usual this morning, and the idea of grabbing his own caffeine fix seemed charming in the orange light of the sunrise, so he'd allowed himself the impulse. A good businessman has instincts for when breaking habit is in his best interest, and Mark's instincts were proven right yet again when he pushed into Café Sterna and immediately caught sight of Anna Adamos.

She was perched at a bistro table. Her brunette hair was highlighted golden in the rising sunlight and as radiant as ever. She was with a young man, a boy, really, and they seemed to be caught up in conversation. The boy said something, a wry twist to his lips, and Anna responded with a sympathetic tilt in her brow.

Mark made a note of the lack of baked goods on their table and made his way to the counter. He ordered his coffee to go and a chocolate croissant, heated and served on a plate. As he waited for his items, he kept his attention on the oblivious pair.

Anna had always been a stunning creature. Mark had known her family since she was a child, and her beauty had only grown as she matured. It wasn't something that was immediately evident, however. She was handsome enough to look at, but it was her intelligence and wit that truly caught your breath.

To see her from across the room was to see any other woman with money; she had confidence and knew how to dress and act. However, to speak with her, to *watch* her speak really, was to watch the shift and play of passion. It sparkled in her eyes and drizzled off her lips. It followed her graceful gestures and crowned her brow. Mark never had to hear what she was saying to know that she was knowledgeable in her subject matter and cared deeply. And it was always a joy to watch her speak so.

Her companion didn't seem to be pulling that passion out of her, but her quick mind was obviously at work somehow, evident in her shoulders, tilted over the table, and her shifting grasp on the mug in front of her.

The barista called his order, and Mark went to collect it. Ceramic plate and paper cup in hand, he strode across the café. As he approached, he saw Anna lean back in her seat and sigh, saying, "I suppose I can respect that." Her tone was more conciliatory and understanding than upset, and he had every confidence in her ability to turn the conversation around if she truly couldn't stand the concession.

With his usual impeccable timing, Mark took that moment to place the croissant in front of the young woman, saying, "If memory serves, you have a weakness for sweets."

"Mark!" her tawny eyes sparkled as she caught sight of him.

She rose quickly, and their hug was one of familiarity rather than formality. Mark was proud of that achievement. Anna had been slow to warm to him, understandable when they had met when he was thirty, and she was only ten. But as she had blossomed as a young woman, a young professional, he had worked to make himself something of a mentor and secondary father figure to her. Someone to trust and admire. The work wasn't done, however.

Mark had spoken with Anna's father not long ago, highlighting the fact that she had just celebrated her thirtieth birthday this spring and was still unwed. The conversation had gone just as he'd hoped. He had started the exchange with familial concern, stoking a fire that had previously only smoldered in his long-time friend.

Once the fear had gained a good head, he'd taken the next step: the turn, as any well-handled business deal goes. Mark backed off and tried to calm his friend by trying to speak hopefully of her situation as a similarly unattached person. He played his hand so gently that his friend almost hadn't connected the dots himself. But Mark's concern had thankfully been short-lived, and even better, he had walked away successfully and with Anna's father supporting the idea of the two of them coming together more *intimately*. In fact, Mr. Adamos had already given his blessing to Mark's future proposal.

Anna turned towards her friend, and as she did, Mark stepped back out of her arms, putting himself too close to the boy for him to stand up for the introductions. The older man looked down at him and extended a friendly hand as Anna started speaking.

"Phillip, this is a close family friend, Mark. Mark, this is Phillip. He lives at one of the properties my company is trying to acquire."

Mark smiled down at the boy, shaking his hand before turning back to Anna. "Ah, I see! I was wondering what brought you all the way out here!"

It explained who the kid was, as well. This meeting had been business. His business, to be precise. Mark had asked Adamos Realty not to divulge *who* was trying to acquire the Wesley land, but he knew that the owner was a young man in his twenties. *This* young man was in his twenties, apparently.

Anna's smile had always made her eyes glitter, and this expression was always a welcome sight. "My first time in Stardade," she replied warmly. "But what about you? What brings you here?"

"Business, I'm afraid. No sight-seeing tours for me."

Her smile was still tilting her pink lips as she sat back down, gesturing to the boy. "Phillip has been kind enough to allow me to sample the local cuisine as we chatted."

"How kind of him," Mark grasped the kid's shoulder in praise. "Although it seems he neglected to mention the best part. Café Sterna makes the best chocolate croissants on the island. They're baked in-house if memory serves."

"They're actually made by one of the Astiri residents, Granny Hamal," the boy interjects, "and she brings them each morning. But they are the best around."

Mark hums in reply, noting the boy has either misplaced his razor or is unaware of one's use. Or perhaps he both owns and knows how to use a razor, but he was hoping the state of his jaw might detract the casual observer from noticing the purple-blue bags under his eyes.

"Phillip and I were discussing my travels and the different kinds of real estate deals I've helped broker," Anna's voice was gaining a stiff edge, her passions growing with the mention of her company.

"Of course," Mark nodded, always eager to see her in her element. "Have you told him about the deals you observed in Morocco?"

He had taken her along with him when she had still been in university and only dreamed of building what she had now. It had been a week of beaches and boardrooms, and the twenty-year-old had been absolutely giddy with gratitude.

"It hadn't come up …" Anna trailed off, her plush lips twisting slightly.

Mark was about to fall into describing their trip to Phillip when his phone started to ring. He pulled it out and looked at the display before sighing.

"My apologies, but I'm afraid I'm needed," he said to Anna. At her nod, he smiled and took his leave.

"Rand," he answered the phone, stepping out of the store and onto the street.

"Mark!" It was his COO, Tim. The man rarely called, but when he did, it was always important. "I'm calling with a few questions about our plans for the Wesley land. I've just had a chance to look at the reports Isabell compiled, and I wanted to re-confirm what we had decided with this new info."

Mark stopped walking to better concentrate on what his partner was saying, as he hadn't had an opportunity to look at Isabell's reports yet. His business administrator had been tasked with surveying the population and aggregating the data to give them an idea of what sort of battle the company would be heading into around this new dig site.

He glanced around to make sure he wouldn't be overheard, but he had turned at the corner and left the crowd on the main street as he'd answered. Now, he had nothing but blank walls and opaque windows to overhear.

Mark and Tim's conversation wasn't a long one, and the CEO sipped at his coffee with satisfaction as they quickly reached a consensus.

"Yes, I don't think it's in our best interest, at the end of the day," he agreed. "I understand that our schematics for the mine place the slag heaps close to the island's historic district, but Stardade's laws are clear in our rights to place the waste anywhere we deem appropriate on our legal property, environmental impacts not-withstanding. That location is the most cost-effective and efficient, and moving in a different direction will slow us down and waste more money. We keep the plans as they are. If the community is really *that* concerned, we can donate to a local museum or something to win back favor."

Tim readily agreed, and they ended the call not soon after. Mark tucked his phone away and adjusted his cuffs before continuing his walk back to his car. He was happy he'd had a chance to see Anna, but he couldn't wait to be off of Astiri. The island had its charms, he supposed, but its infrastructure and cuisine selection were sorely lacking. He had to make do with off-brand sparkling water, for Heaven's sake! He was eager to get back to Valtross and civilization.

Chapter 7

The Situation

THE DRIVE FROM the café to the ferry was a short one, and Mark was soon giving cash to a narrow-eyed worker who stiffly handed him back his change and ticket. Mark simply nodded and rolled up his window, driving forward cautiously. It was like that with these people, sometimes. The occasional Stardade citizen would recognize him, and their whole demeanor would change, growing cold and suspicious or sometimes even fearful.

The country had just settled down from a civil war not six months ago, so some suspicion of outsiders was understandable. But some of Stardade's media had been looking for someone to blame for their hardships and decided to target him, a successful businessman working in, but not a citizen of, their war-torn country.

Multiple articles had been written drawing connections between the Rand Mining Corporation and various political figures. None of those articles had come from any *reputable* news sources, of course. Mark had made sure, and even less authentic information had found its way out of the small, backwater country. But the rumor mill had still done its work, and the occasional semi-literate hick could pair his name and face with the media's lies.

Mark guided his car into the front of the valet line and handed over his keys, ensuring he had all of his valuables in his briefcase and nothing was left in his vehicle. He knew the other passengers weren't allowed down by the cars once they boarded the ferry, but he wasn't certain how much the ferry workers were paid, and he didn't trust them not to make a stupid decision if he left something tempting in the back seat. He only wished he could take the car stereo with him. But no, that would be too obvious an object to steal. Common sense would have to be his best defense in that arena.

Once his car was purring happily on the path into the bowels of the watercraft, Mark made his way to the stairs to see how much space was left on the upper decks. Every time he was forced to make this trip, it seemed more and more worth it to purchase a helicopter and build a landing pad by his main office on the island. Rand Mining was a successful business and growing every day, but he tried to make it a goal not to make such extravagant business expenses for personal reasons. If any of the mines on this little spit of an island were big enough to warrant the transportation of clients or interested partners, he could justify the purchase, but that wasn't the case currently. Perhaps, with the acquisition of the Wesley lands, he could finally make it happen. In the meantime, he'd have to share his space.

As he found a place to sit, Mark's thoughts circled back to what Isabell's reports had said about the locals' hesitancy in his company's expansion. He had every confidence it wouldn't pose an issue to his people. The end of the civil war had seen quite a few positions in Stardade's government filled. He had ensured those government positions now contained people sympathetic to Rand Mining's particular interests and growing pains. The convenience of his puppet placements didn't yet trickle all the way down to the local government of Astiri. But he didn't think the process would be difficult should he need to fill those gaps.

The media might have blamed Mark and a few of his compatriots for their previous president's unfortunate death. But they couldn't give a detailed enough picture to hold any legal water. These claims were all from fanatics and tinfoil hats, as far as any judge and jury were concerned. After all, Mark was skilled enough to orchestrate the disposal of an indifferent, democratically elected leader and install his own hand-picked replacement. Ergo, he was sure supplanting a mayor would be laughably simple. Really, he needed only to wait for Anna to follow through on her plans and then follow through on his own machinations with Anna. If all went as predicted, he would be well on his way to an early and happy retirement with a ludicrous nest egg and a beautiful wife to nest with.

When he got back to his office, he would make a call to the Secretary of Commerce Talmadge Clark in Stardade's capital of Altairazed City. During an easy conversation with Talmadge, Mark would make sure he was scheduled for lunch with the president's Cabinet next week. He was already planning a trip to Stardade's capital city in a few weeks, so it wouldn't be too difficult to bend a few ears at the same time. Perhaps, if Talmadge showed enough promise in this task, Mark would even take him out for a work lunch and give the young man a few pointers.

He and Tim had picked the Clark kid out of the crowd, recognizing his political shrewdness. Talmadge had an unfortunate lack of connections due to his low birth, but it never hurt to have an ambitious and talented young man in your debt. What's more, if Mark ever sensed any weakness in the kid, he would be more than happy to act as his mentor and confidant. Talmadge might never rise beyond his current Cabinet position in the Stardade government, but even pawns could turn the tide of a chess match if used cleverly enough. Mark had no qualms with pushing this pawn to a sacrificial position to benefit his own position. And Talmadge was in a decent job with enough political influence to bend the Stardade president's ear.

Mark settled back happily in his seat on the deck of the ferry. He listened to the crowd murmur and jostle around him. He could be patient. It had paid off before, and it would again.

From his inside suit-coat pocket, he pulled a small, red-velvet box. Opening the box, he admired the ring in the sunlight. He had purchased this engagement ring for Anna a year ago—at a steal of a price, too. A Stardade refugee, who had fled to Valtross, needed quick money when the war still raged with no end in sight. The refugee had mumbled something about this ring being his grandmother's, so it "must go to only your one truest love." Mark had agreed, assuring the man he would put the ring to good use. *My truest love is money, and Anna's hand will indeed serve the purpose of my one truest love.*

Mark always carried the engagement ring, as prepared as any businessman worth his salt ever was. The cobalt-infused silver band gave off a blue hue. The 1.5-carat round diamond would catch the glimmers of blue in the sunlight and send the color sparkling over Anna's delicate hand. The elegant, classy jewelry was sure to stun and dazzle the moldable young woman into saying *yes.* And he had only purchased the best for the future wife he hoped to please. Well, he hoped to keep her happy so that she would be malleable to the whims of his business mind. Together, there would be no limit to their business ventures. The power couple could rule all of Valtross. Their influence could expand into Stardade, then all of Africa, then the whole world over.

As his plans with Anna percolated, he would fill his time ensuring his hold on this small, benighted country's government saw to his company's needs first and foremost. *What is a country, after all, without a robust economy?* He snapped the jewelry box closed. *And what* is an economy *without fair trade? Well … trade, anyway.*

Chapter 8

The Call

"THIS IS TALMADGE Clark, Secretary of Commerce to the Stardade President's Cabinet," he answered his office phone after the first ring. "How can I be of service to you?"

"Talmadge, my boy! It's Rand," his booming voice said through the receiver. "Why the hell are you still using your full title when you answer the phone? My God, man. That was a mouthful!"

"I thought it sounded professional—"

"Frankly, it's beneath you to answer your phone at all, dear boy."

"My own office phone?" Something about talking to this man always made Talmadge feel defensive like he had to prove himself at all times—like he wasn't worthy of even talking to him or being in his presence.

"Don't you have a secretary?"

"Well, yes, but—"

"Forward all your calls to her. You'll thank me."

"I'll discuss the matter with *him*," he said, his patience wearing thin, "but why did you call, Mr. Rand?"

"Ah, right. I need to call in a favor." Not the first time he'd said this line. There seemed no end to Mr. Rand's favors. "Set a lunch date in downtown Altairazed City with the Councilmen Baldrige, Walters, Dankworth, and me in the next week or so."

"For what time, sir?" He jotted notes as they spoke.

"To my knowledge, the councilmen prefer an earlier lunchtime. Let's say eleven?"

"I will check their availability."

"Set the meeting as urgent, Clark. This matter cannot wait."

"Will do. And what shall I state as the title of the meeting?"

"Just our names will suffice." Papers rustled on the other line.

"I see." He chewed on his pen, an old nervous habit. "And what shall I list as the purpose?"

"Never you mind that, old sport." Rand forced a chuckle. "We'll handle the matters of housekeeping."

But I'm handling the housekeeping matters by setting the meeting, Talmadge thought. He said, "Understood, Mr. Rand. Should I call you directly if I have any questions or concerns?"

"Just reach out to my secretary," he said, sounding distracted.

"I'll forward you the details once they're settled."

"Very good, my boy. I'll look for the email by this afternoon."

"I'll do my best."

"Make it happen, Clark." His voice sounded stern before he hung up.

Talmadge set his phone on the receiver at the corner of his modest desk. Looking around his closet-sized office, he reflected on how poorly that conversation had gone. His eyes fell to the thin, closed door beyond which his secretary, Bill, sat at his side-table-sized desk. The Cabinet member dismissed the idea of forwarding his phone to Bill's line. The secretary already had enough on his plate, handling all of the office keeping and business management of the team of Cabinet members.

His gaze fell to the physical map of Stardade on the pine wall to his right. The map, woven into a tapestry as large as the wall, detailed the landforms and bodies of water with exquisitely crafted artistry. Though the tapestry was expensive, it was worth every cent, especially as the only decor he placed in his office. The topographer, an elderly gentleman who'd made a thirty-five-year career of mapmaking, had sold him the tapestry at the local weekly craft fair and farmer's market. In hushed tones, the seller had explained how he always worked to emphasize the beauty of the natural landforms in his work. He chose his words carefully, paying mind not to relate any discussion of land to the politics that had sent the country into its civil war. The elder's conversation aimed to stay light for more than the purpose of etiquette; many of the governments' current laws prohibited affiliation with the dissolved Unimona Party. One warning sign that pointed to a sympathizer, according to Talmadge's law seminar, was their overemphasis of their love for the nation's landmasses. On the bustling Altairazed street, Talmadge held the map, unrolled like a sacred scroll, and noticed that the topographer hadn't bothered to color-code the cobalt mines, as many modern maps did.

During the war, Talmadge had studied at a university in London, experiencing his own separate peace from his country's turmoil. However, as a Stardade citizen, he had kept up with the news alongside his studies. From a distance, he had read detailed analyses, both foreign and domestic, about the Unimona Party and Nasaw Parties' diametrically opposed opinions. He would never tell a soul that he disagreed with the dismantlement of his country's freedom of speech. With the good of the people in mind at all times, he felt minority groups needed a voice in the government. In fact, Talmadge had signed on board for this job with the intention of making a difference in the lives of people like this man, his fellow citizen.

Besides, Talmadge enjoyed taking his office phone calls himself. He always fancied himself a people's person. He put his pen back in his mouth. Setting aside the businessman's briskness and condescension, Talmadge let the implications of the conversation sink in. He looked at his notes and wondered, *Why doesn't he want me to know the purpose of the meeting?* Pulling the pen out of his mouth, he tapped it on the legal pad of paper. Little flecks of spittle littered the names. He reflected back on Rand's involvement in his own placement in the Cabinet.

He had an awful flashback of scrolling through his phone while at a bistro table at his favorite coffee shop one afternoon. As he took a second bite of his bagel, he received a news alert about the former president's appalling assassination. The bagel turned to ash in his mouth, so he washed it down with bitter coffee. Before he could even finish reading the article, Rand called him to congratulate him on his promotion to secretary of commerce. Up until that moment, he had thought the businessman had simply planned to put in a good word for him. As a wealthy business owner in the mining industry, of course, Rand had connections in the Stardade government. Apparently, he also had connections to hitmen willing to shoot the president during a tour of the country. The truth tasted like bile on his swollen tongue.

As he looked at the legal pad of the councilmen's names, the secretary of commerce tasted that same bitterness. These were the very same men he had met during his first week working for the new president. He knew who they were and what they stood for because Rand had hand-picked these businessmen for a meeting with himself over cocktails. Rand introduced them as "our inner circle" and "men we can trust." They had come out of the woodwork of Stardade's wealthy class.

Typing on the computer in his tiny office, Talmadge accessed documents easily at any Presidential Cabinet member's disposal. He could access a number of classified documents due to his high-level security clearance. He pulled up the head council's latest meeting minutes and the men's résumés, which displayed little to no political experience. Baldrige was a stockbroker invested in Rand Mining Corporation; Walters was a political activist who'd been born into money, which he invested into the Nasaw Party; and Dankworth was a professional gambler and previous manager at Adamos Motor Group.

With his pen in his teeth, he looked through a number of articles about the council's involvement in the Nasaw Party. Their influence on several megacorporations, including those run by Rand and the Adamoses, had oiled the gears of monopolizations that had forced locally owned businesses into bankruptcy. *If Rand is gathering these men for a clandestine meeting, nothing good can come of this encounter,* he realized. *This meeting is to plan another coup d'état.*

"But for whom?" he wondered aloud. "And how can I put a stop to this?"

Extracting the pen from his mouth, he reached to deposit the writing utensil in his pen cup, which he knocked over. Pens, pencils, markers, and highlighters, scattered over the desk like a broken rainbow.

And that moment was the straw that broke the camel's back for Secretary of Commerce Talmadge Clark. *I can't owe this man any more favors. He* thought as rage licked through his chest, consuming his heart. *I can't do this job anymore.* Looking at the desktop of his computer, he saw his saved background of the Sidras Mountains on the horizon of Astiri Island. *This country and its people are why I pursued this career, not to be some dastardly businessman's henchman.* Panic struck him as his shaking hands went to his face. *But I'm in too deep. How do I get out? I have countless files on this very computer that a court could use against me.* His hands fell to his keyboard and mouse once more.

"That's it!"

Talmadge swept his desk clear and dove into a drawer to extract an external hard drive. He got to work making copies of the most damning documents he could, saving them all to his personal flash drive.

Chapter 9

The Breakdown

JAQUELINE STARED AT her phone as another text came through from Phillip. Her friend was in the middle of blowing up her phone for the third time in two days about some Valtross bimbo who had gone to meet him yesterday and had gotten herself stuck in the valley.

Her phone pinged again, and she sighed, staring at the first line of the text long enough for the screen to go black before lighting up with a fourth message. Normally, when Phillip was this worked up, it was fun to watch him spin. Jaq sort of made a game of it, finding different ways to poke him, winding him tighter and tighter, until he got so frustrated that he'd spin out, ranting and raging around a room, yelling about the injustice of this or the indignity of that.

Time and time again, Jaq would just sit back and watch, fascinated by how deeply this normally placid boy felt about political issues. And the words he used when he was mad were so wildly different from how he normally spoke. It was comical! Somehow, when Philly got mad, he *gained* vocabulary points. Weird, Shakespearian ones. He'd spout off about lily-livered scuts and people's spleens for some reason. She still had a few videos of some particularly spectacular rants saved on her phone.

The same phone that just lit up with yet another text.

The problem wasn't that her friend was upset. The problem was that he was upset about a girl. A woman. A very successful, adventurous woman. Who was probably pretty and classy, and everything Jaq wasn't, with her sweaty workout clothes and memories of teenage acne to overcome? She had been so frustrated to get such a grumpy reply from him outside the coffee shop. His comment had been about the lack of variety in coffee shops, too, which he had never seemed to mind before he met *her*.

Her phone pinged again, and she turned the ringer off but couldn't look away from the screen as it glowed and dimmed. And glowed and dimmed.

She had read the first message.

I just finished coffee with Anna, it had read.

Anna, he'd written. So familiar already. *One* business coffee and they were on a first-name basis.

Well, more than one coffee, she supposed. One coffee and one night spent doing who-knows-what when "Anna" had gotten herself a free night at Phillip's house.

Was that how they did things in Valtross? Did the businesswomen just throw themselves at anyone proving to be a challenge, then climb the ladder feet-first?

God, was that coffee even really a "business meeting" or whatever like Phillip had said when he'd brushed her off that morning? Or had he taken "Anna" out for coffee as some sort of post-sleep-over thank you?

Her screen flashed again, and she couldn't stop herself from reading.

God, Jaq, I don't even know …

He didn't know what? Didn't he know how to carry on a long-distance relationship with his new Lady Love "Anna"? Didn't he know that he was slowly crushing her heart, falling in love with another woman when he already had her, trussed up and in bows, waiting for him to notice her? Didn't he know that Jaq would give him whatever he asked for if he'd just give her a chance? Didn't he care that she was the CPA of her family's firm who was set to inherit the company? Didn't he know she was an absolute catch? He should give *her* the opportunity to blow his mind while "stuck in the valley for the night" and prove herself worthy of a coffee in the morning.

Jaqueline needed to take a shower. She'd just gotten home when Philly had started using her phone as a strobe light, and she still stunk to high heaven after her morning run. She'd gotten as far as her bedroom on shock-numb legs. But she needed to do something before her anxiety spread further, and she ended up staring at the wall in a panicked stupor for an hour.

Jaq plugged her phone into the charger and thought about flicking the sound on again, but quickly changed her mind, shoved it under the pillow on her bed, and practically ran into the adjoining bathroom. She turned the water on high and stripped off her sweaty gear before plunging under the still-frigid water. She gasped shakily as her hair slowly plastered to her neck and face.

Phillip might get wound tight about situations. Jaq might have been able to push him to the point of raving when they were in high school. She knew what buttons to push by asking him about deforestation or deep-sea fishing, or the evils of monoculture. But he *never* let *other* people get him to this point. Her Philly was *above* investing in other people to the point that another person made him angry that badly, that person wasn't worth his time.

Or that used to be true.

Phillip had only met this woman yesterday. Could she really have changed that much about him? Didn't people only change for the people that they loved?

Well, theoretically, he'd never been in love before. Could someone fall in love in a day?

Jaqueline used to think she wanted to live in a world where love at first sight existed, but she hadn't realized that reality could be quite so exquisitely painful.

God, and if that was true, why couldn't it have been *her?* She was pretty! She liked all the same things Phillip liked. She was even learning how to cook more than canned soup! Hell, she was the only one who knew about that time that Phillip had been scared out of his car at a red light by a huge spider. He had tripped over the curb on the side of the road and somehow face-planted into a pile of dog poop! And *she* still found a way to love him despite it. Because of it. Because it was a part of him that wasn't so pretty, but he had still chosen to share this part of him with her.

Screw it.

Screw. It.

If some random *Jezebel* (thank you, Phillip) wanted to try and take her man, she wouldn't find the process quite so easy.

Jaq shut off the shower with a slam and whipped her towel off the rack beside the tub, plans already forming in her head for how best to win Philly's heart.

She wasn't giving this one up without a fight.

Chapter 10

The Manipulation

PHILLIP GRABBED FURIOUSLY at his hair and turned in his pacing around Jaqueline's small living room.

"God, Jaq! I don't even know what I was thinking or how I let myself get my hopes up! I knew—*I knew* that every single member of *that* family was a sack of mealy worms feigning being a human! They're million-aires from *Valtross,* for Heaven's sake! How could I have been so stupid?!"

He'd come here hoping the comforts of an old friend would help cool his anger, but the more he talked about it, the more angry he seemed to get. The venting wasn't working in his favor.

"She pretended to listen, you know? The whole time, she pretended to listen to me lecture her on the sins of her country and the struggles of mine. She even pretended that she understood some of it. Acted like I was changing her mind about some stuff, even!" Phillip's hands were back in his hair as he swung around yet again to take the three long strides to the other side of the room and about-face. "*She* gave me hope! She deserves a gosh-darned Grammy for her performance, too. I bought it!

Unwillingly, *unwittingly*, naively, took the bait hook, line, and sinker."

Jaq was sitting on the couch with a pad of paper and a pen, and she was doodling something in the margins of a list she was making. This had been their go-to positions when one or the other wanted to rant: one spectator, one angry pacer. It had worked for them in the past, but, somehow, Jaq's almost clinical calmness made Phillip's anger worse.

She sighed and dropped the pen onto the pad as she looked up at him. "Phillip, you're being too hard on yourself. We know those people are basically Hellspawn, so of course, they'd have some sort of temptress minx in the mix."

That made Phillip pause. *Temptress?* he considered. *How had Anna tried to tempt me?* She'd played him, sure, but she'd been straightforward in what she'd offered. Even when he was drunk, she practically tucked him into bed and ditched him. After saving his life, no less.

"Temptress?" he asked.

"I mean, yeah? Wasn't she playing the whole 'Damsel in Distress' schtick with all her 'Please, Mister, I'm in danger. Let me sleep over' tactics with you?" Jaqueline specified in a drawl.

"*What?*" Phillip's mind raced as he tried to see things from Anna's perspective. Had Anna tried anything like that? Yeah, she'd agreed to stay the night, but that was only after Phillip had insisted. And he'd felt something with her, sure, but she hadn't batted her eyelashes or anything like that. Even when he had drunkenly commented on her hair—a stupid moment that he figured he could never erase from his mind—she had insisted he go to bed.

"Come on, man, you can't seriously tell me you don't see it," Jaq said. "A known land developer—"

"Broker," Phillip cut in. "She's interested in old municipal buildings and updating older architecture with eco-designs to upgrade them without taking from their grandeur."

Jaq paused and studied Phillip for a moment, her eyes tracing his face before she leaned back in her seat and started to twirl a lock of her red hair between the fingers of her right hand.

"So you say," she conceded. "But how much of that is the truth, and how much of it is tailored to sway your opinion?"

Phillip felt his chest constrict a little. Was that true? He thought back to their conversation in the café before it all went to Hell in a Valtrossian, high-fashion handbag. She'd seemed earnest. Her eyes sparkled when she talked about what she had seen on her travels and what she hoped to accomplish with her company. Could that have all been a facade?

Jaq smiled sadly at him. "It's hard to know when someone is manipulating you when you're such an honest person. That's what I admire about you, Phillip. You put your heart out there and assume everyone else does the same."

Phillip rolled his eyes in response, continuing his pacing. "Whatever, Jaq. I'm not certain she was faking all of it, but you know who was? Her friend *Mark*." Phillip felt poison dripping from the name as he said it, and the sensation gave him the strangest mix of feelings. He got the distinct impression he was acting like a seventh-grader but hating that deplorable man held so much catharsis he couldn't help the behavior.

Jaq's smile was shark-like, and Phillip returned it with a smirk of his own. *This* was familiar ground.

"Oh? Do tell," she prompted, settling back into her seat and picking her notepad and pen up again.

"*Ugh*, where do I start? You won't believe me anyway. This man was like a walking, talking Shakespearian villain, I swear to God. I wouldn't be surprised if he greased back his hair with his own motivational speeches in the morning. Iago has found his match, and it is Mark Rand!"

Jaq was snickering on the couch, her pen writing furiously.

"Seriously, Jaq! We were just sitting at this table having a perfectly fine conversation when this … this cockalorum walks over, puts one of Granny Hamal's croissants in front of her, and says something like 'Don't you like sweets?'"

The voice Phillip puts on makes Jaq laugh even harder, curling over her pad of paper. Her response receives an answering smile from Philly, but he doesn't stop. He is on a roll now.

"After that, he basically ignores me, except to look down on me or continue to force Anna to have a conversation with him. She was visibly uncomfortable, but this absolute mooncalf didn't pick up on it, and he just kept going!"

"*Mooncalf?!*" Jaq's eyes are squinted shut with laughter and she's waving her hand in the air. "Mercy. Mercy! You have to give me a minute!" She's still laughing between words, and Phillip can't help but chuckle.

"Seriously, Jaq! He just kept blathering on about business *this* and Morocco *that*. I'm just happy he didn't suffocate himself due to lack of breathing between sentences."

"Oh gosh, I can only imagine," her laughter has died, and she's wiping tears from her flushed cheeks.

"You don't even know ...."

"But Philly," her eyes are still glittering with mirth, even as she gives him a sly look. "You should be happy you met him, even if he was a major creeper."

Phillip felt his mouth twist in distaste, but he waited for her to explain.

"If you hadn't met him, you wouldn't have known who was talking on the phone about your property. You would never have realized Anna was lying to you."

Phillip rocked back on his heels at that. Put so plainly, the realization was hard to stomach. He'd been so sure Anna was being honest with him. *Especially* after meeting Mark. He had seen her put on a mask around her old "friend" to keep him happy, even as he completely ignored her numerous hints that he should leave. If he could see through that acting, why had he fallen so hard when she'd played him?

"Yeah ..." he said, voice quiet and regretful. "Yeah, I hadn't thought of it like that."

"Oh, Philly!" Jaqueline stood up quickly, padding over with her arms out and a pout on her face. "Don't look like that! You're making me sad."

Phillip accepted the hug but stepped away after a moment. He suddenly didn't want to be with Jaq anymore. He didn't want to be with anyone. Well, that was a lie. He desperately wanted to talk to his older brother Matthew, but that wasn't likely to happen, barring a ghost encounter. The hole that had opened in his chest six months ago seemed to grow just a little, and a chill took any remaining laughter he had.

"Jaq, I'm gonna head out," he heard himself say, voice still subdued. "I'll catch you later, okay?"

His friend looked at him in concern but nodded her head, following him to her door. She caught his wrist before he left, and he turned, meeting her green eyes.

"Phillip, take care of yourself, okay?" she said, eyes serious. "No more toaster disasters."

Phillip mustered a small smile and nodded his head in assent before turning and heading back to his truck. *If Anna wasn't there for the toaster disaster,* he considered, *I wouldn't be here to talk about her at all. I'd be talking to Matthew in the afterlife.*

As he got into his truck and drove away, he wondered if Anna could really be all that evil of a person when she had saved his life. If he had died, the estate would have gone to auction, as per Stardade law. Then, Mark could have swooped in and easily bought all of the land.

But instead, she had saved him, along with his family's home, when he was being drunk and stupid. He knew he was prone to the unfortunate habit of drinking too much when he wanted to resist making a big decision. *I miss my family. I'm certain they would agree I should* not *sell the land.* He turned his truck up the dirt road towards home. *But what would they have to say about Anna?*

Chapter 11

The Apology

THE MOLTEN LIGHT filtering into Jaqueline's kitchen spilled through the sheer curtains to fill the sink and glint off the hardwood floors in ruddy splendor.

Jaq sighed and stirred a spoonful of sugar into her coffee as she admired her familiar surroundings. She'd been on the fence about buying this house until she saw the kitchen. The house itself wasn't much to look at, but the kitchen was airy and woodsy, and the window over the sink had a charming, if modest, view of a small pond and pasture that bloomed with wildflowers in the spring. Anna wasn't a cook, but she had fallen in love with this room. It had given her a feeling of warmth and home that had reminded her of Phillip.

She took a sip of her coffee and hummed in satisfaction. Jaq sat back on the cushioned bar stool at her island and thought about what had just transpired.

After Philly had left, she'd relocated to the kitchen for a much-needed, late afternoon caffeine fix. But the hot coffee and golden view didn't seem to be able to melt the shard of ice that had settled into the pit of her stomach. Had she pushed Phillip too hard? She hadn't thought so at the time, but she'd never seen him like that before. Not about a person, anyway. He'd been absolutely livid, to the point of yanking on his hair. She'd wanted to stoke the fire and get him angry at Anna so he'd dismiss her, but had she gone too far? She'd only wanted Phillip to realize that Anna was just another woman, just another rich floozy from Valtross out to make a buck. But thinking back on how he had reacted to everything she had said made her second guess herself.

"We know those people are basically Hellspawn, so of course, they'd have some sort of temptress minx in the mix."

God, the look on his face. Like Jaq had stepped on his childhood hamster or something. He had looked confused and distressed, and the expression would have been funny out of context. But knowing she had been the one who had caused that reaction just made her slightly nauseated. And then she had doubled down with that whole "Damsel in Distress" label that she had hammered home with "Please, Mister, I'm in danger. Let me sleep over.". *Those* comments had not gone well. Anna had tried to shift his perspective, and instead, she had gotten a lecture on Anna's hopes and dreams. What even was that? He'd known this woman for all of forty-eight hours, and he suddenly knew her whole backstory.

Jaq huffed in annoyance and sipped at her coffee, but the ice in her heart wasn't going away. She had tried to steer Phillip away, but thinking back on what she had done, her behavior wasn't sitting right. She looked down at the pad of paper she'd brought with her. The paper featured her list of Philly's insults. In the margin, she had her own artistic renderings of a stick figure she imagined looked like Anna being drawn and quartered. She stared at her doodle as she thought about what else she had said to Phillip.

"It's hard to know when someone is manipulating you when you're such an honest person. That's what I admire about you, Phillip. You put your heart out there and assume everyone else does the same."

The words seemed to echo accusingly in her head. *Hard to know when someone is manipulating you. Is that what I am doing?* Was she manipulating her best friend? She only wanted what was best for him. She didn't want him to get hurt, but she had never met Anna. Phillip might doubt his own ability to read people, but Jaq trusted his intuition implicitly. If he'd come to admire Anna, that wasn't something to be tossed aside lightly.

And Jaq knew her words held weight with her friend. Phillip might be guileless, but they both knew Jaq could read a room, as well as Philly, could see a person's true intentions. "You're such an honest person," she had said. She had praised him for this quality, even. And he was! But who was she to say she admired that about her best friend if she wasn't able, to be honest with *him?* Maybe she couldn't be honest with everyone, but she had known Philly since they were kids, and she was toying with him when he was upset.

And *god*, somehow, she kept forgetting he was still in mourning! Phillip's brothers were all so much older than him. Jaq had never seen much of them. She had grown up with him, but she had never really interacted with his other family. Somehow, that meant that she had temporarily forgotten that he had lost them *all* less than a year ago.

Phillip had been devastated. He hadn't left his house for a month. She had made sure he ate, even if all she could make him was scrambled eggs or Cup Noodles. She had nagged him into keeping relatively clean. But what if she hadn't been there?

Jaq dropped her face into her hands and groaned with shame. How could she have tried to manipulate him? Phillip had come here, obviously hurting, and she had only made claims to further her own agenda, forcing a wedge between him and Anna.

She just found it so hard to remember that he still wasn't okay. He had been a disaster that first month. But after that, Phillip pulled himself together. He had insisted Jaq had her own activities to do and that he didn't need babysitting anymore. After that, he seemed fine any time she saw him around town. Somehow, that situation had translated to her utterly forgetting how fragile her friend still was.

God, she really was the absolute worst. She loved Phillip for all the same reasons she hated herself. Where he was innocent, she was manipulative. Where he was bold, she was conniving. Where his patience stemmed from care for others, hers stemmed from calculation. Phillip deserved better than her. He deserved better than this Anna girl, too, but there wasn't anything Jaq could do about that. All she could do was come clean and beg Phillip to forgive her.

But she needed to offer him more than just an apology. Philly's favorite food was strawberry cake, but there wasn't any place you could buy some on the island. The season was, however, the height of spring and, thus, strawberry season. Jaq pulled her phone out and started looking for a recipe. She might have trouble boiling eggs, but she had the whole weekend ahead of her, and the grocery store was a five-minute drive from her house. She was going to make this cake. And then she was going to give this peace offering to Phillip and tell him everything that was going on. Next, she could only hope to God he still wanted to be her friend at the end of her speech.

Jaqueline was determined to make herself worthy of her best friend. Even if he couldn't see himself with her romantically, she loved him, no matter what. She couldn't even remember life before she had met Philly.

She took a deep breath and steeled herself.

Even if Phillip would never see her as a romantic partner, she needed him in her life. She hadn't done a good job of acting like a best friend, but she could change that. She *was* changing that.

Selecting the recipe with the highest rating, Jaq picked up her pad of paper. She tore off the top sheet of paper with the list of insults. *I am turning over a new leaf.* Grabbing the pen, she brushed off the new sheet and began her grocery list.

Chapter 12

The Realization

THE WHOLE FERRY- ride back to the mainland, Anna replayed in her mind the conversation she'd had with Phillip in the coffee shop. *Sure, I've always known Mark wants the land for mining,* she considered, *but would he really devastate the historic district with garbage?* From the back of the boat, she watched the island shrink in the distance. The greens of the trees blended into the blue-green of the South Atlantic Ocean.

The farther she drifted from the island, the more she felt she was leaving her heart behind. Phillip had been right when he had commented on her powerful emotions regarding the view from his house. Obviously, the land was breathtaking, like a mountainous, fairytale forest. More than that, though, Phillip had hinted at her kindling awareness of a feeling beyond her current understanding. However, she could not ponder out the reason why a realization in its most basic form took root. If she wasn't mistaken, being in Stardade, on Astiri Island, she had felt like she was home.

As she drove off the ferry and onto the dock, she wrestled with the idea of calling Mark. As she drove from the beach to the highway and went north, she got lost in her thoughts. She didn't doubt that Phillip had overheard Mark's conversation on the phone. However, she wondered about the validity of his interpretation based solely on his eavesdropping. Yes, Mark's conversation was not meant for Phillip's ears, but apparently, Mark had made a couple of suggestions that might not have been for Anna's ears either.

She'd had no idea about the mining operation's waste disposal plans. She didn't care for the tedious discussions on mining that never failed to come up in her social circles. Yet, the little she did know about mining meant that she knew cobalt was a byproduct of mining other minerals. Of course, this meant that the mining company sold the worthwhile products to other interested companies. Also, the whole process produced waste, to her knowledge, companies disposed of this waste legally and in a way that followed international protocol. *Every activity Mark has always been above board, right?* Anna was second-guessing the businessman's intentions, along with his morals.

After thirty minutes of driving, she crossed into her country. She showed her papers to the border control guards. Then, she continued along the international highway. She couldn't help but notice how much better paved Valtross's side of the same road was compared to Stardade's side. On her home soil, she realized she needed to talk to someone—well, a couple of someones—way more urgently than Mark. Before she could confront that businessman, a supplier, she needed to speak to the source of the cobalt demand. She needed to talk to her parents.

The night before, Phillip had brought up countless points about the morals, including the environmental impact, of the Adamos Motor Group. Among the sins of her family's company, he had explained the lack of sustainability in their business model. Meaning, unbeknownst to her, the Adamoses were violating one of her core beliefs: protect the Earth. She prayed none of these details were true, that Phillip was mistaken. But a prickling suspicion in the back of her mind told her that his points might have had validity. She would have to bone up on the facts by reading several reliable sources. Before she started that process, though, she needed to talk to the person she always talked to about her problems: her dad.

Another thirty minutes had passed since she had crossed the border. Back at home in her capital city, she navigated to her parents' city estate. Despite a full couple of days of meetings and travel, she felt this discussion could not wait until the morning. *I hope to god we aren't on the wrong side of this deal.*

⚯

"But of course, our company favors sustainability," Anna's father said as he sat next to her on the sofa, his whisky neat in hand. "The whole point of us making electric cars is to support the environment."

"Yes, darling, isn't that quite obvious?" her mother contributed from her armchair before sipping her dirty martini.

"Sure, of course. That's not really what I'm asking about." Anna braced herself as she took a sip from her glass of water. "I'm wondering about the *mining* company's environmental policies. The mining companies that we—you—hire to extract cobalt."

"Oh." Dad cleared his throat. "We don't concern ourselves with the mining procedures other than to confirm through legal advice that all mining, especially international mining, is done to the letter of the law."

"So, what you're saying," Anna started thinking out loud, "is that you don't know."

Mother offered a jingly giggle as she waved her hand in dismissal. This move was an obviously practiced gesture that Anna had seen her do at parties. "Darling, we don't need to know. We aren't miners. We're a car company."

Anna felt her cheeks heat at her mom's flippancy. *I'm not an idiot,* she thought. *I know what my family's company does.* After a sigh, she said, "Of course, *Mother.* I was just startled to hear—from a foreigner no less—that the company's morals are questionable."

"Questionable!" Dad guffawed and put an arm around his daughter. "Not at all. Everything *we* do and that the companies *we hire* do is one hundred percent legal. This isn't about morals, tiger." He squeezed her shoulders. "This is about business."

"And business is booming." Mother raised her glass.

"Cheers to that!" Dad raised his own glass.

They both sipped as Anna riddled out the deeper meaning of their words.

"Time for a refill," Dad said, taking both his and his wife's glasses to the bar.

The Adamos Motor Group hired miners—mainly in Stardade—to bring cobalt home to Vlatross. Those mining companies followed Stardade's laws, environmental or otherwise. So, Mark's plan to dump waste in the historic district of Astiri was legal. Alternatively, he was involved in illegal activity, and her parents didn't know. Though she considered the possibility that her parents were lying, she doubted the plausibility. Since its inception, the company had always operated legally. Of this, Anna was certain because she used to sit in on board meetings as one potential heir to the company. *I need to talk to Mark,* she realized. However, she had a few more questions for her parents.

"Speaking of which, how did your meeting with the Wesley boy go?" Dad said, his back to her as he mixed the drinks.

"Oh, yes." Mother sat at the edge of her seat. "Tell us all about it."

"He's not a boy," Anna said to Dad's back. "He's only a little younger than me."

Her mother raised her eyebrows. "Okay?"

"I'm still working on it," Anna said, examining her glass of water. "That's why I wanted to talk about all this."

"That's my girl." Dad turned back to the ladies. "Always does her homework. What's on your mind?"

"I know our government supported Stardade's government throughout their war," she said. "When the Unimona Party rose up, the Nasaw Party declared civil war. Correct me if I'm wrong. Adamos Motor Group contributed both money and vehicles to the Nasaw Party, right?"

"Why the sudden interest in politics?" Mother asked, receiving her refilled martini glass from Dad.

"Linda, our Anna has always been interested in politics." Dad sat back down next to Anna. "We've had countless debates, haven't we, tiger?" He sipped from his full glass.

"Yeah, we always have. But am I right?" Anna asked.

"Yes." Dad nodded. "Where is this going?"

"Why did our family's company support the Nasaw Party? You all just make cars."

"Why, money, of course." Mother laughed again before sipping her martini.

Dad chuckled, too. "She's right, to be quite frank. If the Unimona Party overtook the government—and had their way with it—we'd never see another nugget of cobalt from Stardade."

"But why?"

"The Unimona Party considers the environment—as well as its *socialist* practices—a top priority." Dad's disdain for socialism was clear in his tone; Anna had always known his preference for capitalism and disgust for its counterpart. "That being said, if the filthy rebels had taken over, they would have run all international miners out of the country. Then, honestly, our company wouldn't have stood a snowball's chance in hell."

"So, as co-presidents of the car company, you two chose to support the international, free market."

"You got it, tiger." Dad bumped shoulders with Anna. "The Nasaw Party knows the importance of the economic stimulation our company provides. Without us, Stardade is just a hunk of minerals. Without Valtross,

Stardade is the equivalent of a man finding hundreds of diamonds while stranded on a deserted island. Without an economy to sell those diamonds into, that man has no wealth at all. Just a bunch of pretty rocks."

"Oh, I see." Anna sipped her water. "So, I know logistically how the Nasaw Party won, like the battles and key dates, et cetera. But how did they convince the working class, those not in the Unimona Party, to join their cause? I know their rise in popularity is what won them the war."

"Simple," Dad said. "A well-oiled propaganda machine. The government showed the working class the merits of rallying behind the Nasaw Party."

"And what were those merits?"

"What everyone wants, darling," Mother said. "To make money."

"Is it really that simple?"

"Sure, and why not?" Dad said.

"The working and lower classes would have benefited from the government reform that would've provided welfare, like universal healthcare and social security."

"It doesn't take much work to teach an uneducated class of people that socialist ideals, like the ones you mentioned, are evil. The government simply gave its people a nudge back in the direction their country had already been following.

"The well-paved road to continued capitalism."

"Bingo, tiger."

The ugly truth materialized before her eyes. The Nasaw Party's leaders—and my family's company—wanted to continue making money. The leaders knew their propaganda machine could convince even the working class—the largest demographic in the country—to continue to support the wealthy. All the while, the rich convinced those workers that they supported the greater good. But the only ones getting rich off the Stardade government's continued control were the wealthy. Wealth begets wealth. *And my family's company is the Nasaw Party's ally.* Anna sighed and leaned back on the sofa. *Our country supported this party's continued power.*

Chapter 13

The Spiral

THE SUN HAD basically set by the time Phillip pulled into his usual parking spot at the foot of his house's hill. Normally, the drive up to his property was something he enjoyed. Getting to watch the eaves of his house peak through the trees and over the hills as though the home were greeting him usually soothed any irritation he might be feeling. The sound of crickets and small frogs would ring like a bell tolling his happy arrival. This time, though, he was too distracted to notice the welcoming environment of his home. Thoughts of what he had overheard, and Jaq's opinions on the matter, running through his mind took his attention away from his surroundings.

Stepping out of his car and into the dimming evening, Phillip slammed the truck's door and marched up to his house. If he was going to keep thinking about Anna, he might as well clean up after her. He unlaced his boots at the door and trod up the stairs on socked feet, pushing the door to the room Anna had slept in open abruptly. *This was Matthew's room.*

The bed was still mussed. The white cover glowed a faint blue in the dying light of day. The sheets were creased at the side facing the window, the edge was thrown open to the view as though the previous occupant were inviting the mountains and stars to cradle them until they fell asleep.

Phillip wondered if Anna had been stargazing before the fire alarm had called her out of bed last night. Did she know the constellations, or would that be something he could teach her? Lying in the cool grass, side by side, he would trace out Orion in the sky. She would laugh at him, tell him she didn't know anyone who couldn't find his Belt, at least.

Phillip shook himself and roughly stripped the cases off the pillows. After that, he disassembled the rest quickly, and he threw the whole bundle down the stairs, listening for the satisfying *fwump* of its landing.

She lied, he reminded himself. None of what had happened was true, nothing he felt was real, and he'd had the right impression of who she would be before he had even met her. He had just been distracted by a pretty face; that was all.

He double-checked that the rest of the room was clean and nothing was left behind, then he trotted downstairs after the sheets to start the washing. He was shoving the bedding into the washer when he remembered Jaq's cool voice repeating words like *Hellspawn* and *temptress minx.* Something about those descriptions didn't sit right in Phillip's gut, but lately, not much had been sitting right.

His whole family was dead.

His whole country was run by some gutless puppet.

His family's land was being poached by billionaires with the intention of ruining the entire island.

Who was he to say what sat right?

With a sigh, Phillip started the washer and wandered into the kitchen, looking for the last of the Scotch he'd started last night. He found a clean glass and poured himself a finger, sipping at the drink over the sink.

Come to think of it, he'd read a few articles about how Mark Rand had some suspicious connections with the current president. One piece he had read hadn't said anything outright, but some of the connections it had drawn still sent a chill down Phillip's back when he thought about them. After meeting the man, he couldn't say he would put assassination past him. And if that were the case, what would Rand do when Phillip refused to sell?

Phillip considered his glass and poured himself a healthier amount, taking the glass and the rest of the bottle with him into the sitting room. Settling into an armchair by the empty fireplace, he took a larger sip and hummed in satisfaction at the burn as he swallowed.

His situation had never gotten this bad when he was a kid, but whenever he'd gotten tangled in something stupid, he always used to go to his family for advice. His father had been a rock, and his calm had helped steady Phillip when he would start to spiral. Often, his insight helped make even the messiest situation seem simple to fix, and that would give Phillip the courage to see it through. On the rare occasions, his dad hadn't been able to do that, Phillip would go to Matthew or his mom, and they would help take the problem off his mind. The both of them were a pair, ready to tease anyone and quicker to accept a jab with good grace and bright laughter. Phillip's brooding was never able to stick around for long when he was with them.

Phillip went to take another sip and realized he'd drained his tumbler while he'd been thinking. He refilled it and pressed the cool glass to his cheek as he stared out the floor-to-ceiling window at his mountains. How was he going to get out of this situation? A way out seemed impossible. And even if getting out *was* possible, solving the problem seemed like an awful lot of effort to go through. Was it worth all that? Saving his own life?

He wouldn't sell the property, but he got the distinct impression that saying no to Mr. Rand wasn't always a survivable experience. If that was the case, maybe it was for the best. He would get to see his mom and dad and brothers again. He would get to sleep without nightmares and get to actually *rest*. He wouldn't take his own life, but maybe this way, he could make his parents proud and still be allowed to let go. It would devastate Jaq, but she was strong. She'd survive it … losing him …

The sound of his cell phone ringing drew him out of his haze, and he looked around for it. He had to put his empty glass down to reach into his pocket and pull out the phone. Blinking blearily at the screen, he saw an unknown number flashing back at him. Swiping to answer, he pressed the phone to his ear.

"'Lo?"

"Phillip? Is that you?" Her voice sounded heavenly.

"Anna?"

"Um … yeah …" came her hesitant reply.

Phillip just groaned in response. "Seriously, Anna? *Really?* Would you just leave me alone? I already told you I wasn't selling—"

"No, Phillip, wait!" Her voice held something like panic, and Phillip paused long enough to allow her to regroup. "Um, I'm not ... I'm not calling about the property."

Phillip just grunted, unwilling to trust her with more than that.

She sighed, pained, but kept talking.

"I, uh. I spoke with my parents. About, ah, about Stardade and Valtross's history and stuff."

"Congratulations."

"Spare me the sarcasm, please. I know now."

"And what do you *think* you know?"

"After I spoke to my parents, I did some digging. I read up on Stardade and Valtross's tenuous relationship. Turns out you were right."

"Course I was right!" He hiccupped. "About what was I right this time?"

"Are you drunk?"

"None of your business, *Miss Adamos.*"

"Okay, clearly, you're not in any state to listen."

"What gave me away?" He hiccupped again.

"Right." She sighed on the other line. "Well, I understand much better where you're coming from now. I called to apologize."

"*Well,* you can take that apology and shove—"

"Phillip, please, just be aware that I plan to talk to Mark Rand tomorrow. I'll get to the bottom of his plans for your land."

"I knowed—knew—it!" Once again, he hiccupped. "You're in cahoots."

"That's not—*Look,* I will speak to you tomorrow. Just don't try to cook anything tonight, okay?"

"Ha!" He hung up before he knew if his laugh was sarcastic or not.

Setting the phone on the end table next to his chair, he looked up at the staircase. He took a moment to ponder whether he had the energy to stumble up the stairs, then fell asleep in his chair.

When Phillip hung up on her, Anna took a deep breath, then set her phone down on her condo's kitchen island. As difficult as this was, she would need to give the drunk estate owner space to rest and sober up. Hopefully, the next day he would be willing to listen.

Looking out the sliding glass doors that made up one wall of her kitchen, she watched the twinkling city lights. The nightlife in Prijipati City provided quite the view from her condo overlooking the capital. Earlier, the sunset had darkened the beach view off in the distance. She worried Phillip was too stubborn to let go of his vendetta against Valtross's involvement in the war. Clearly, by extension, he blamed her family for the war and his personal loss. Since he overheard Mark's supposed mining disposal plans, Phillip also blamed her for his troubles.

All along, she had done her best to make Phillip like her. In real estate, making a purchase or a sale often depends on how much a client likes you. For some reason, though, she cared less about the land acquisition and more about Phillip's opinion of her. Once she knew about all of the inner workings of this land deal and what it meant for all the stakeholders, she'd be best able to assess what to do.

But first, she had to gather all of the puzzle pieces to this picture. And the picture was turning out to be much bigger than she could have ever imagined. Though she wanted to storm over to Mark's house, bang on the door, and sort out his true intentions, she thought better of it. Arriving at his house at this hour would catch him off guard. Not to mention, that move would be unprofessional, and Anna prided herself on her professionalism.

Instead, she put on the kettle to make herself a cup of tea. She needed something to soothe her nerves and knew honey and lemon juice in some chamomile usually did the trick. After such a busy couple of days, she needed to rest and gather her thoughts. And a good, clear analysis always started with a good night's sleep.

Even though Mark was a "family friend," she needed to keep him at arm's length. He was a businessman and, quite possibly, a slimy one. For this reason, she decided to pick up her phone and send him a quick calendar invite, rather than a call or text, to set up a meeting tomorrow. No matter what his intentions were, this ordeal was a business transaction. Sure, she wanted to help her family out; of course, she wanted to land this deal for her real-estate company. *But at the cost of what? Where do I stand in all of this?*

The whistle on the tea kettle squealed. As her tea steeped, she mulled over her feelings. Her entire life, she had had a passion for the environment. She even gathered a fundraising and volunteer group to plant trees for her sixth-grade science project. Of course, her parents had always ingrained in her the importance of electric cars in the global energy crisis. Even all of her municipal building renovation designs included ideas for sustainability and the incorporation of nature. *One of the reasons I love to repurpose the old buildings is for the sake of reducing human waste.* She pulled the teabags and mixed honey, with a little lemon juice, into her tea.

Her phone chimed. Mark had confirmed that he would attend their meeting at his office tomorrow morning.

Anna enjoyed her hot tea, then got ready for bed. *Just like Dad says, a good night's sleep works wonders.*

Chapter 14

The Prospect

RAND MINING OFFICES were more utilitarian than grand. Where some choose to wow potential clients with luxury and surplus in their headquarters, Mark chose to take a quieter approach with his business. Money might talk, but wealth whispers, and while he never wanted for anything in his main office, no part of the design boasted as much. His company rented the tenth and eleventh floors of a skyscraper at the edge of downtown Prijipati. As such, his office had a wonderful view of the city skyline lit up in the ruby light of the rising sun to help sweeten the taste of his morning coffee.

Mark sat back in his chair with satisfaction, curling into the plush leather seat as he watched his city wake up. His hand went to the ring he kept in his coat pocket, as it often did these days. It seemed the thought of marriage made him sentimental. He opened the box and pulled the jewelry out to inspect it in the red light, the morning sun glittering across the facets and planes of the main diamond. He thought of Anna and what a suitable wife she'd make for him. He thought he might propose to her soon. She wasn't the romantic sort, his Anna, so he didn't feel the need for much wooing. He'd frame their partnership as more of a business transaction, benefitting her and her company in a multitude of ways. And she would be his jewel, his beautiful, brilliant, young, and vibrant wife to help entertain him and brighten his days in his upcoming retirement. Mark smiled in satisfaction, shut the box with a snap, and safely buried the ring in his pocket. He'd ask her over a nice dinner after the acquisition was complete.

Comfortable with this decision, Mark finished the rest of his coffee and sat up in his chair, turning to begin his day's work when his secretary buzzed in, letting him know the very woman occupying his thoughts was on her way in.

"Mark, thank you so much for meeting me on short notice," Anna exclaimed as she glided into the room.

"Of course, my dear. You know I'll always make time for you." Mark stood up, walked around his desk to embrace Anna, and led her to the couches surrounding a coffee table. "Would you like anything to drink? Coffee or tea, perhaps?"

Anna smiled sweetly up at him and shook her head, "I'm fine, thank you. I don't want to keep you from your work for long. I just had a few questions I needed to ask you about the Wesley land."

"Of course, dear! Ask me anything. I'm an open book. I need to be to help you help me, after all!"

"I heard a rumor that your current plans place your waste close to the historic district on the island. Is that true?"

"Ah!" Mark leaned back, placing his hand along the back of the couch and crossing his legs. "Is that it? Yes, I'm afraid so. The evils of drawing up blueprints before you're able to properly survey the land."

"Evils?" She seemed relieved when she said it. "So, you know that putting it there runs a risk of runoff and other waste materials ruining the district?"

"Yes," Mark hummed. "An unfortunate reality, that."

"So, you have your people working on rewriting the blueprints since you know what a disastrous effect it can have on the environment and people nearby?"

"Rewrite?" Mark barked out a laugh. "Dear me, no! Do you know how much money that would cost us? Worse, do you know how much time we'd waste trying to fix every little problem like that?"

Anna sat up a bit straighter at that, her shoulders set. "Little problem? Mark, people *live* there. Phillip is already unsure about selling his land because he cares about the environment, but this…."

"*This* is smart business, Anna. You're young, so you don't quite understand fully, but nothing you build will ever be perfect. It's a problem with building it in the human world. There will always be problems, always be someone getting hurt, there will always be waste and runoff, and it has to be put somewhere. My job, as the owner of this business and the leader of my people, is to ensure none of those things are a threat to *us*."

"But Mark, there's a difference between things not being perfect and people's homes being slowly rotted because of a slag heap!"

"I know, I know," Mark patted Anna's knee consolingly, as he had done when she was a teenager. She'd had a penchant for pouting over silly things on trips. "The reality of running a company is never as clean as one thinks it will be getting into it. I understand this is a hard thing to confront, and I'm sad you're forced to struggle with it for the first time on one of my projects. But I'm afraid the Hallmark of a good CEO, as I know the both of us are, is to never back down from such struggles. We must always persevere and keep our end goal and our companies in mind."

Anna quietly contemplated Mark's words for a moment, her head down, gaze focused on her lap. Mark allowed her the time, remembering his own struggles early in his career when he thought he could smooth over every issue as she now did. Finally, it seemed she acknowledged the wisdom he was imparting. She looked up from her lap and offered him a shaky smile.

"I'm embarrassed to have been so naive," she said with a slight blush.

"Not at all, my dear. You show grace in recognizing the wisdom of others and ceding the argument."

She shifted slightly, and a new determination seemed to grow as she cleared her throat and continued. "Well, if we're to get our hands on the Wesley land and truly start this, I should brush up on Stardade legalities. Do you have someone in your legal department that might be able to help instruct me?"

"Of course, that's a wonderful idea! We have a paralegal who's compiled a rather thorough knowledge of the matter. If you ask my secretary to bring you down there and ask for Andrea Lex, she should be able to help you."

"Thank you, Mark. I really value your expertise in this matter," Anna said sweetly, standing and offering him a handshake in farewell. Always so composed, his Anna. Mark saw her to his door and helped get her sorted with his secretary before making his way back to his desk and booting up his computer for the day.

She really would make the most exquisite wife.

Chapter 15

The Intel

YUCK! ANNA THOUGHT when Mark's secretary left her in the hall outside the paralegal's office. *That sorry excuse for a businessman could not be more vile if he tried.* At least she'd had the opportunity to make herself proud with her acting skills. Mark had seemed to fall for her ruse hook, line, and sinker. In truth, she was enraged at his callous revelation that he couldn't even pretend to care about the Astiri historic district. *That man doesn't know the first thing about me if he thinks I'd side with the destruction of history and nature in favor of "smart business."*

Phillip had been right when he had interpreted the conversation he had overheard between Mark and his COO. She had to contact Phillip—who would hopefully be sober by this hour—to let him know. But first, she had to finish her intel-gathering mission.

She knocked on the office door of Mark's primary paralegal.

A woman's cheery voice said, "Come in."

"Hello," Anna said as she opened the door. "My name is Anna—"

"Adamos!" She stood to round the desk and shook Anna's hand. "What a pleasure."

"Are you a fan of the Adamos Motor Group?" Anna said, shaking the other woman's hand.

"Not exactly." She let go of the firm handshake to tuck a strand of hair behind her ear. "I've followed Adamos Realty since its inception. Your charity events and bold, sustainable designs are the talk of the town—well, at least in my circles. You use Scandinavian architecture techniques if I'm not mistaken?"

"That's right," said Anna with an authentic smile. "You must be the first fan I've met outside of a business meeting. Your name is Andrea Lex, correct?"

"Yes, that's right. Andrea Lex, at your service." She indicated the chair in front of her desk. "Please, sit down."

"Thank you, Miss Lex." Anna sat down.

"Please, Andrea is fine." The paralegal sat behind her desk. "How can I help you today?"

"Well, I just met with Mr. Rand about his potential land acquisition in Astiri."

"Oh, the Wesley Estate?" She clicked on her keyboard. "I have the file here."

"Yes, the same one. Mr. Rand and I were discussing the, hmm, *consequences* of him buying the Wesley Estate for the purposes of mining."

"You mean the plans for the waste, don't you?"

Anna nodded, leaning forward.

"Between you and me," Andrea whispered, "I think the whole thing reeks of questionable morals." She returned her tone to normal. "But, rest assured, there's nothing legally wrong with his waste disposal plan. The miners will gather the waste *near* the historic district—up the mountain from the area—not *in* the historic district."

"Really?" Anna crossed her legs and sat back in the chair.

"Unfortunately, that's God's honest truth. It's also true that the runoff from their waste will undoubtedly impact the historic district. But the law doesn't protect against *potential* runoff, especially where mining is concerned."

"I'm just. Hmm. Well, I'm just surprised his business doesn't need to acquire the historic district to move forward with these plans."

"To be straightforward, a business cannot purchase the historic district."

"Oh." Anna leaned forward again. "No?"

"No, the historic district is protected federally. In fact, it's part of the Stardade National Park System."

"Please, Andrea, tell me more about that."

Chapter 16

The Hangover

PHILLIP'S PHONE BUZZED on the end table next to his chair, waking him up. The lamp was still on next to him, but the valley outside was dark. He sat up and rubbed his hands over his face. Not only were his eyes crusty with sleep, but his stubble was scratchy on his hands. *I'm hungover again.* When he reached for the phone, a crick in his neck twinged from the awful position he'd slept in the chair. *I gotta stop drinking so much.*

He answered the phone while massaging his neck. "Hello?"

"Phillip? This is Anna." Her elegant, professional voice came through the phone crystal clear.

He had a sense of déjà vu. A feeling of warm comfort at hearing her voice spread through his chest like honey melting into hot tea. "We talked last night."

"Yeah, the conversation was brief." She said flatly. "Listen, we need to meet. This is important. How soon can you be at my office? I'll text you—"

"Hold up. Slow down. I need a sec." He cleared his throat and rubbed his temple with his free hand. He would never admit how much he liked to hear her telling him what to do. "Okay, so what is this meeting about? The land?"

"Yes and no. Look, I really can't say too much over the phone. Trust me?"

Though Phillip was not ready to trust her, he would allow her this meeting. He could tell from the urgency in her voice and words that this was as important as she was claiming. But he loathed the idea of going to Valtross. Not to mention, he felt in control when he hosted on his family's estate.

"One condition," he said.

"Name it."

"You come here. Today." He looked at the time on his phone and allowed himself a few hours to get ready. "Ten o'clock *sharp.*" He remembered he needed to shower and shave. "No, come at high noon. Don't be late!" *Now, who has the high ground?* he thought smugly.

"I'll get to you as soon as humanly possible," she said on the other line, voice a mix of irritability and patience. "I already know how to get to your place anyway." Her keys jangled as she picked them up.

"See you then."

"Mhm." She hung up.

Freshly showered, shaven, and caffeinated, Phillip stared through the back windows of his house. Luckily, sipping water since he'd woken up had curbed his headache. The pills he'd taken after eating some cereal probably helped, too. Though the hour was well after noon, he couldn't fault Anna. He had picked an arbitrary time while grumpy and didn't even know how long it would take to travel from Prijipati to Astiri. Still, he wished she was here already. Feeling antsy. He observed a flock of birds fly from the top of the mountain down toward the beach. *What could she possibly have to say to me now?* he wondered. *Did she meet with Mark?* He sighed, feeling frustrated.

Even though he expected it, the knock on the door startled him.

Phillip opened it to Anna, a tiny ball of energy looking adorably flustered.

"Thank you for inviting me," she said.

"Come in, come in. Can I get you anything?"

"Honestly, I could use some chamomile tea if you have it."

"Not a problem. Let's go to the kitchen."

Phillip prepared them both some tea to take to the living room to drink. Meanwhile, Anna poured her heart out. He listened silently to every word, sipping his tea as his mind steeped in her words. She admitted her previous ignorance concerning her parents' involvement in the shady dealings with the mining companies. She revealed that Mark had admitted his plans for the Astiri Island Historic District. She even explained how she now understood Valtross's involvement in the Stardade Civil War. Then, she claimed she had a surefire way to protect all of the Wesley Estate's land.

"I need your help, Phillip, but you aren't going to like it," she finished.

Though he didn't know why he felt a pang of excitement at the prospect of Anna needing his help, but he was wary about what that help entailed. He examined the remains of his tea at the bottom of his mug.

"You have some sort of plan." He looked up into her brown eyes, which twinkled with hope. *Hope,* he realized, *not mischief.* "This plan will protect my land. And you need my help."

"Yes." She set down her cup. "We can memorialize the Wesley Estate. We can declare this land," she pointed to the view outside, "protected as a historic landmark."

"We?" He offered a skeptical look.

"You can do it on your own if you want." She reached over to take his rough hand in her soft one. "But I know the bureaucratic process to memorialize *and protect* your land. You just need to gather evidence that your family loved this land."

"Wait, bureaucratic?" He pulled his hand out of hers and crossed his arms. "Sounds like we've hit the part I'm not gonna like."

She put her hands in her lap. "I know how you feel about—"

"But you don't. How could you possibly know my feelings? Have you ever grieved a day in your life? Have you ever experienced profound loss caused by *your own government* and its dealings with a foreign nation?"

"No, I haven't. And words could never begin to describe how sorry I am for your loss. But, Phillip, *I* didn't kill your parents. And *I* wasn't directly involved in that civil war. All I can do is help *now.* All I can do is try to make a difference *now.*"

Phillip looked from her gleaming eyes to the glorious view. He couldn't help but catch a glimpse of Anna reflected in the window. She sat at the edge of her seat, legs crossed and fingers fidgeting.

"You clearly need some time to think about this," she said. "And I haven't had the opportunity to see the little hidden gems of this beautiful land. Would you like to get some air together?"

"That's not a bad idea." He set down his own mug and stood up. "As much as I love the hiking trails, my favorite spot on the whole island is the garden we have out back."

The two went through the back door of his kitchen and down the outside stairs. Nestled amongst the trees, they followed a sand trail for a little while in silence. Phillip loved how sweet the air smelled up here. A bird chirped in a tree above them, and a second bird echoed at a higher pitch. Sunrays filtered through the canopy, casting scattered spots of the forest floor in gold.

He realized how romantic this forest was for the first time in his life. Countless times, he had roamed this land, exploring with his brothers and Jaq without a care in the world. Before the civil war blew their life to bits, they had all been naive children playing. Now, alone with Anna, the land felt different, less childish, and more mature.

He looked over at his companion to see awe glimmering on her face. Her lips parted as she took in the scenery. Her big, brown eyes took in the surroundings as her cheeks grew rosy with emotion. This immersion in nature seemed a wake-up call for this person who had perhaps been sleeping in a concrete jungle her entire life. She looked like she belonged here like she had only come into her true from here, on this very land. He then realized he was looking at a woman who had fallen in love. She had fallen in love with Astiri Island.

This meeting wasn't some final ploy. Some move to make a play for the land acquisition. In fact, this plan was the opposite. Yes, he would have to come to terms with giving the land to the government and the Nasaw Party. However, once the National Park System took over the area's protection, nothing short of an act of God could harm the estate. He knew this protection held weight for a fact. As a prominent estate owner, he had closely followed the news, policies, and laws concerning land acquisition matters. He couldn't believe he hadn't thought of the idea first. Clearly, grief (and another substance) had been clouding his judgment.

"Tell me about your home," he said as they walked. He wanted to know more about her, especially after they had spent so much time talking about his home.

"Ha! It's incomparable to here." She swung her arms wide, taking in their surroundings.

"Please, elaborate. I've never been outside of Stardade."

She let out a slow breath. "It has its merits in its own right. The buildings are impressive and quite beautiful. They're a little too modern for my taste. It's busy and loud, which is fine. It's just what I've known my whole life. While I'm out here, though," she raised her hands above her head, seeming to praise Mother Nature, "I just feel more centered. I feel like I can actually hear myself think. Sometimes, visiting any big city, I wonder if all of civilization's progress is worth the cost. That question has only become more prevalent as I've learned what my family's industry has done just from mining. After I left you the other day, I did some deep-dive research. I'm not gonna lie, and this next part is hard for me to admit. But you made me realize that no matter how informed I thought I was, I only viewed the tip of the iceberg for my whole life." She looked at him as he felt pensive about the changes he'd seen in this woman in just a few short days. "Sorry, I've blathered on a bit." Her cheeks flushed. "There's just something enchanting about this forest, I guess. Like I could confess all, and nature would forgive me my transgressions, those I committed knowingly and unknowingly. Does that make sense?"

"It makes perfect sense," he said, brushing a hand over her back to ease her concerns about his opinion. He didn't expect the way touching her would make his fingers tingle and his head become light. His hand fell to his side as he saw her cheeks turn deeper red. "Mother Nature, she's—How do I put this?—a forgiving entity. In fact, I'd say she's more forgiving than any of us deserve. But she knows our true intentions and where our hearts lie. At least, that's how I look at it all."

"That's a wonderful sentiment." Her smile, part relieved and part joy, caught him off guard.

His reaction to looking upon her gorgeous face was like how he had felt when he had touched her back moments ago.

"You know," he said. "You didn't have to set this meeting. You didn't have to give me this National Park idea."

"I needed to."

"What made you decide to help me?"

"It's pretty simple, really. I know I have to do what's right. And it took me a little while, but now I know what's right."

"You do know your parents won't be happy if they find out you're helping me keep this land unmined." He could hear the waterfall rushing close by.

"I need to take a stance on this." She shrugged. "Heck, let my family cut me out of the inheritance for all I care. I don't want their dirty money."

Phillip chuckled, feeling a weight lift from his shoulders.

"Wait," she said as they stopped walking in front of a thicket. "Did you make a decision about the land?"

"You know, I think I did." He felt an authentic smile touch his lips. "Let's do it."

"Yes!" She jumped up and down, clapping her hands. "Can I help you complete the process?"

"Of course. I need you to help me protect this …" He moved aside some vines and opened the tall, wooden gate he had constructed as the entrance to his family's secret garden. "After you."

Anna stepped over the outdoor threshold. He admired her beauty as she spun to look around, her arms wide. The elated expression on her face hinted that she felt she had stepped into a magical world. A thicket, dense enough to act as a natural fence, bordered the small clearing in a roughly rectangular shape. Various colorful patches of flowers decorated the garden floor to the left and right, in blues, purples, reds, and pinks. Though he had not tended the garden in the past six months, the place had a wild, overgrown quality he admired. Mother Nature reigned here, as majestic and in control as she intended. The flowers had blossomed, spread their seed, and prospered while untouched. A stone path dotted the middle of the man-made meadow, encouraging people to walk a road less traveled. The occasional flower or vine grew over the stones. The path led to the crowning jewel of the garden. No higher than one story, a flowing waterfall fell from the cliffside of a hill and into a small pond at the garden's far end. From the pond, a creek flowed through the thicket and out of sight. The water's rushing and babbling provided a natural white noise, making the area feel like a little slice of paradise. The hand-crafted wooden bench that Phillip had made rested in front of the pond, facing the water.

"Who did all this?" Anna turned to ask over the sound of the moving water. She stood in the middle of the garden within arm's reach.

"It was a team effort, really," he said, feeling the spray from the waterfall. "My whole family. We all cleared the plot. I did the woodwork." He pointed to the bench, then the door. "Matthew and Dad did the walkway. Mom and Ethan planted the flowers."

"This place is so beautiful!" Her cheeks were flushed with excitement.

"You're beautiful," Phillip said.

Anna closed the space between them with two short steps and took his face in both hands. He bent down to kiss her, their soft lips colliding as their bodies hugged close. He closed his eyes and saw starbursts behind his lids. His strong hands held the small of her back, pulling her as close as possible. Surrounded by the sweet smell of nature and her floral perfume, he tasted her honey-sweetened lips. Her small body was a little furnace against him as her delicate hands caressed his smooth face and into his hair. A tender moan escaped his lips as she licked his tongue. He ran his hands up her back, losing himself in her powerful presence. She whimpered in pleasure as he tangled his fingers in her hair. They explored one another's pent-up passion with their mouths. Neither had known just how much they were missing before this shared moment.

Chapter 17

The Sunset

AS THE TWO kissed, consumed by their passion for one another, Anna felt joy ignite her entire being. Low in her stomach, a longing tingling spread warmly to her extremities. Phillip's firm body pressed like a shelter against hers. He smelled of piney shaving cream. She could taste the spicy tea still lingering on his tongue. Her heart galloped like a wild horse, her pulse racing with uninhibited freedom.

Swept up in this scene out of a dream, she realized how magical this moment was compared to other kisses she'd had. Hidden in the surreal garden and enclosed in his strong arms, she felt her past dissolve. Presently, Phillip didn't care that she came from shady money or that she had so much to prove to him about her authentic concerns for the environment. Here with him, she could just be herself without her last name holding any weight. In the garden, they were just a man and a woman, giving themselves over to the feelings they'd tried and failed to deny.

Phillip slipped his fingers down to the top button of her shirt.

"Wait," she gasped, pulling her face from his.

He moved both hands to her shoulders. His blue eyes licked with excited flames, but he awaited her next move.

She looked at his lips, considering what she wanted. More than anything, she wanted him right here on the forest floor. But their relationship was complicated at this juncture. Though he had decided not to sell his land to her damnable client, she still had a responsibility to follow through on helping him with the National Park System's paperwork. She wasn't certain she could complete this job she had made for herself while distracted by her feelings for this incredible man.

"Anna." He tucked a strand of her hair behind her ear. "Are you okay?"

"Yes, I just …" She licked her lips. "I just need us to take this slowly. I need time." She took his hands in hers. "Trust me, I want to take this further, but I need to wrap my head around a few things first."

He squeezed her hands. "No need to explain. Our relationship has started off unconventional, to say the least."

They shared an understanding chuckle as Anna remembered their first face-to-face conversation starting off with an argument.

"Take all the time you need." He leaned down to brush his lips on her cheek and tenderly kiss her skin. He moved his mouth to her ear and whispered with warm breath, "I've waited my whole life for you. I'll wait as long as you need."

His words melted her core, sending delightful heat radiating from her center. All she could manage to say was, "Thank you, Phillip."

"Always." His smile caused her heart to flutter once more. "Let's go back to the house and get something to eat."

The lovebirds left their sanctuary, Phillip shutting the door behind them and hiding it with the vines. Walking back to the house, Anna thought the forest somehow appeared even more vibrant and colorful than before, even though the hour was later than when they had walked in the opposite direction. She noticed yellow wildflowers strewn over the clover-covered floor, growing in patches of sunlight. The creatures, stirring and chirping from their hidden places, seemed more alive, more energetic. The fresh air smelled sweeter, and the hike exuberated her. Her whole worldview seemed to have shifted, reprioritized from one awe-inspiring kiss. *Is this what it feels like to fall in love?* she wondered, looking at Phillip's handsome, kind face. She took his hand as they strolled. He smiled at their fingers, blushing as he met her eyes.

"So, I better confess now," he said, "that I have no idea what food I might have in the house."

"We'll figure something out. I have simple tastes."

"The heiress of one of the world's largest corporations has *simple tastes?*" He raised his eyebrows and smirked, one dimple showing on his cheek.

"What can I say? I'm a simple girl at heart, and you've already pleased me very much."

The red in his cheeks deepened. "You're not at all what I expected, you know that?"

"You're not the only one full of surprises, Mr. Wesley. Though, that garden tops anything I have up my sleeve."

"I'd beg to differ. Your memorialization plan is brilliant."

"You might want to hold your praise until we've made it happen."

"We'll make it happen." His smile could probably stun her every day for the rest of her life. "I have every confidence in your abilities, Miss Adamos."

"Yeesh." She giggled. "I miss when we were on a first-name basis. Let's go back to that."

"As you wish, Anna."

"I love the sound of my name on your lips."

"I love your lips."

She giggled again, heat traveling up her neck and into her cheeks.

"Too much?" he asked, discerning yet playful.

"Not too much, not by any means," she said, shaking her head, "but you've gotta get your head in the game."

"Fair enough." He raised his hands in mock surrender.

Back in the kitchen, they left their shoes by the door.

Phillip took a rushed look in the pantry and concluded, "Yep, I got nothin'."

"Let me see." She stood next to him, gazing with her dark eyes at the ill-matched boxes, cans, and jars. Placing her hands on her hips, she said, "I see bread. Got any cheese?"

"Yeah, but no meat."

"No problem. What about butter?"

"There should be some in the fridge."

"Oh, and I see some tomato soup right here." She pulled out the loaf and can.

"Ahh, I'm with you now. You're thinking grilled cheese."

"Yup, one of my favorite comfort foods."

"Sounds excellent! Brings me back. Haven't had that since I was a kid."

"Haven't—" She lost her voice for a moment. "I'm not convinced any person has truly lived until they've had grilled cheese as an adult."

"Oh, really?"

"It just hits different, ya know?"

"No, I don't know, but I'm happy to find out."

"Let's do it. Got any milk?"

"I think so. What for?"

"Sweet Phillip," she said, slightly teasingly. "You have so much to learn. Show me your spice cabinet."

His cheeks flushed, but his eyes danced with amusement. "I think my mom kept her spices up here." He opened a cabinet. "Aha!"

Within fifteen minutes, Anna had shown him how to make garlic-and-onion grilled cheese and tomato soup with milk, basil, and rosemary. Phillip expressed his delight in the modest dish at the dining room table with hummed satisfaction.

"Where did you learn to make grilled cheese like *this*?" he asked. "It's delicious."

"Growing up, my parents' chef noticed I took an interest in her cooking when I was maybe eight. So, she shared some tips and tricks with me."

"You must have been quite the pupil."

"Funny you say that. I was a rascal in school."

He raised his eyebrows as he licked tomato soup from his upper lip.

"Mhm, that was me, the problem, middle child. Couldn't stand sitting still. I prefer being on the go than working with my hands."

"Sound like you found your stride."

"It took some time, but I finally did." She offered a smile, feeling at home discussing her feelings with him.

"I think everyone needs some time to find their place in the world."

"I agree. Real estate always fascinated me even though my parents wish I would be more involved with their business." She sipped some soup from her spoon.

"It's admirable you're pursuing your dreams." He dunked his sandwich in his soup. "Lord knows I'm still trying to figure out my own place." He took a bite of dripping food.

"If I may say so, you've taken a major step today in figuring out your estate, which is no small potatoes."

He chuckled warmly. "That's fair. I guess I'm wondering what comes next."

"I'm sure you'll figure it out. You have so much passion for Astiri."

"For sure, I do. I need to figure out how that translates into income."

"As a property investor, I found your short-term rental idea worthwhile."

"This is a great spot, right?"

"Definitely!" She took a bite of her sandwich, and they ate in companionable silence for a beat. "Oh, I've been meaning to ask. You mentioned you did the wood-work for the garden. Did you make that sign at the foot of the hill, at the head of your driveway?"

"Yeah, I did. I love carpentry and wood burning."

"Sounds like you were made to commune with the forest and all it has to offer."

"I never thought of it that way." His smile radiated the heat of a hundred stars. "I like that. I feel the most alive out here. And you seem to fit in perfectly."

"Do I?" She tucked some hair behind her ear and felt her cheeks warm. Appreciating his positive viewpoint on how she seemed here, she felt excited to discuss the sensation. "I don't know exactly what it is, but I feel a special emotion when I'm on Astiri. I guess, partly, it's that this place is so different from where I grew up."

"You grew up in the city?"

"Yeah, and I like it just fine. I just didn't know what I was missing before. Do you know what I mean?"

"I know exactly what you mean," he said in an awed voice. His eyes absorbed her face, his gaze like a man watching a sunrise over the valley.

Speechless, her cheeks hotter than ever before, she admired the fine man before her. Without overthinking outside factors, she stood to wrap her arms around his broad shoulders. He scooted his chair back, and she straddled him in his seat. Running her fingers through his hair, his hands on the small of her back, she kissed him. He sighed with delight as she parted her lips and traced his tongue over hers. She tasted garlic and tomato and smelled his pine aroma again. His hands inched up her back, pulling her closer. An excited moan jumped from her throat. She massaged his scalp as their lips and tongues danced. She could feel their hearts racing one another against the inside and outside of her chest. Their intimate embrace enveloped them with warm, delicate passion. This kiss was slower than the one from before, more deliberate, and exploratory.

When their kiss wound down to a conclusion, Anna wanted so much more but still needed time to process before taking the next step.

"If you're interested," he whispered, their noses brushing against one another, "we could watch the sunset. The living room windows face the east, but the opposite horizon of the sunset is still a worthwhile sight."

"Sounds delightful," she whispered back. "The first time I was here for the sunset, I was a little distracted with work."

"It's definitely worth one's undivided attention."

"I don't know if I can offer it my full attention, seeing as I'm awfully distracted," she said, pressing her hips closer to his and enjoying his wide-eyed gasp, "but I'll give it my best try."

"To the living room?"

"To the living room." She lifted her index finger to complement her joking declaration.

To her surprise, he braced his hands underneath her and stood, causing her arms and legs to automatically wrap around him like a spider monkey. He chuckled at her startled gasp. With one more quick smooch, he carried her to the living room. She was awestruck by his strength. Sure, she had seen his biceps and how his shirt pulled taught over his chest, but she hadn't seen his muscles in action before.

"How'd you get so strong?"

"I've chopped a lot of wood."

"Just chopping wood?" She leaned back to examine him skeptically.

"I lift weights in my bedroom when I'm not prepping for winter. I also love hiking, and it's been a while, but I like to run, too."

"I'm a runner," she said, amused to hear they shared a hobby.

Setting her gently on the sofa and sitting down next to her, he said, "We'll have to go running sometime."

"Sounds like fun." She smiled as she propped her feet on his lap and leaned back on a pillow.

He rubbed her feet, causing her to sigh in utter contentment. Her feet hurt a moderate amount from their short hike. The unprompted gesture of affection touched her. In silence, they both watched the mountain, valley, and ocean show off a dazzling, color-changing display. The sky above held scattered orange-tinted clouds. The scene's whites, greens, and blues took on gold hues before deepening in tone. Every few moments, the sight seemed to diffuse a different palette of colors, a particularly emotional experience when coupled with lovely company.

Now and then, Anna would peak at her partner to favor how golden hour cast his stunning form. He looked as appreciative of the scene as she felt. Sometimes, when she looked his way, she realized he was looking at her, too. Eyes on her, his expression was as soft as the clouds drifting above the valley. If she wasn't mistaken, his tender glances showed as much, if not more, appreciation for the sight of her as of the vista. The two shared several soul-gazing moments, cherishing one another. She knew she was beholding a man falling in love with her just as deeply as she was with him.

Chapter 18

The Picture

AFTER THE SUNSET, and a long, tension-filled kiss goodnight, Anna retired to a separate room. She chose the same room she had stayed in the last time she was on the Wesley Estate. Lying in bed, she looked out at the stars and moon again. Though conflicted because she wanted to spend more time with Phillip, she knew she needed some time to reflect. After such an eventful day of travel, research, discussion, and emotions, she found herself needing space. Though he had offered to share his bed with her in the master bedroom, she told him she needed time to wrap her head around her feelings. She couldn't just dive head-first into such a tumultuous relationship with so many moving pieces.

Alone in bed, she lost count when she tried to count the sparkling stars outside the window, and her mind wandered. Over the past few days, Anna realized she had grown rapidly closer to Phillip. Since their relationship had started not only as strictly professional but also with them as star-crossed enemies, she was having trouble processing her own feelings. Their respective family's political and business endeavors were diametrically opposed.

She thought, too, of how she'd had to jump to his rescue when he had drunkenly set the toaster on fire in his own home. His stupidity in the heat of that moment had somehow endeared her to him. She had rescued him as though he was a gallant in distress. Perhaps, the strange event had bonded them or even simply eased the tension in their budding relationship. By the time she had saved his life, their friendship was indeed budding because he had invited her to stay over so that she would be safe from night driving in the valley and mountain bears.

But she would've had to be completely blinded by puppy-dog love to miss the red flags from that first night's encounter. Since then, he had been drunk when she had called him yesterday. That considered, she hadn't seen him drinking in the day or even when they shared a simple dinner this evening. Though she knew little of grief, she knew the process could make people take on odd behaviors. His decision to get drunk while "sleeping on" a big decision, then stumble downstairs and attempt to make toast, had led to a risky situation. She'd also seen him fly off the handle after overhearing Mark at the coffee shop. With just a few eavesdropped sentences, he was so sure she was the enemy he had thought of her all along.

Yet, in the face of all this conflict, she knew she had developed romantic feelings for Phillip. In spite of those tumultuous moments between them, he had opened up, showing trust in her. He had decided to try her plan for the sake of the land that meant everything to him. He had even shown her his family's special garden. She knew he was handsome and endearing and compassionate and intelligent. Sharing the intimate moment in the garden had been the fulfillment of a fantasy she had not dared to fully imagine. And yet, the kiss had been impulsive. She had lost herself in the magical feeling of the secluded place in an otherworldly island's wilderness. Though she had only been on Astiri twice, Anna felt like she was home.

Phillip was so in tune with this land, born and bred on this Stardade soil, that he was part of this land. As a native of the island, he epitomized all that its nature stood for. She couldn't imagine separating her feelings for this place from her feelings for him. The cause and effect were entangled, like the roots of two separate trees, so she could not differentiate the two passions. Though she was unsure how this organic process had begun, she knew her feelings for him, and the land nurtured one another. The two emotions worked symbiotically within her to create a beauty beyond her wildest imagination.

Feeling restless, Anna threw back the covers and turned on the lamp on the nightstand. Though the thought occurred to her, she soon banished the idea of going to Phillip's old bedroom. Because of her mixed feelings, she did not want to feel like she was snooping or crossing a boundary. Choosing a book to read, an old habit she fell to whenever she couldn't sleep, was a safer bet for staying in her lane.

Noticing the bookshelf in the room, she approached the shelves to find reading material. She wanted to distract herself and distance herself from her swirling thoughts. As she brushed her fingers over the book spines, she was surprised that dust didn't come away on her fingers. Then, she remembered that Phillip said he had tidied up the rooms for potential rental guests. *When we succeed in adding the estate to the National Park System, the rental of these rooms could be lucrative for Phil.* The prospect of using her realty network to help him market the rooms excited her. *I'll discuss the idea with him once the dust settles on our plan.*

She set aside the idea for tomorrow, then turned her attention back to the collection of classic British literature on the bookshelves. She remembered this middle bedroom was Matthew's childhood room. The first time she had chosen to sleep here, she'd had no idea why she'd made the decision other than she felt drawn to that room in particular. Hearing the way Phillip spoke about Matthew, she could tell the two brothers were very close.

She pulled a hardcover edition of *Wuthering Heights* by Emily Brontë. Though she had never read the novel, this book was one of many on her to-read list. The realty business kept her busy with little time for her hobbies, like reading for leisure. Examining the cover, she brushed her fingers over the picture of a tree twisted by years of battering winds with the backdrop of a cloud-darkened sky. She could picture herself curled in an armchair downstairs, reading this book. Safe inside on a stormy day, listening to the rain as she relaxed, she'd look up from the novel through the giant windows to see a sky that matched this cover. Phillip would bring her chamomile tea, delivered with a kiss to her forehead, before sitting in the chair next to her. They would chat about the book and his carpentry work, and all the current discussions of politics and property would be settled. The Wesley Estate would have federal protection to remain as nature intended, with its overseers—the two of them a partnership—living right along with the creatures of the valley.

As she opened the novel, the pages parted to reveal a bookmark towards the middle of the book. *Maybe Matthew never had the chance to finish reading this book,* she thought with a pang of melancholy. When she gingerly took the bookmark, she realized it was actually an old-fashioned print photograph. The inked paper stuck to the book's page when she touched the photograph. As gently as she could, she unstuck the square shape. The photo hadn't lost any ink to the page, to her relief.

Holding the picture in her hands, she was careful only to touch the white edge at the bottom so that she wouldn't smudge the photo. Grateful she had erred on the side of cautious handling, she saw the picture featured what was clearly Phillip as a child and an older boy. Their smiles, so similar they appeared copied and pasted, plastered their brotherly features. *This must be Matthew with Phillip,* she realized. As she examined the details, she noticed they worked together to hold up a glimmering silver fish of at least two feet in length. In the background, she recognized the bench from the family garden, which rested in front of the waterfall. The cascading water, frozen in time, backdropped the boys, who stood at the edge of the pond. *What a beautiful memory in a beautiful place.* She was impressed by the size of the fish one or both of them had caught.

She admired the handiwork of the bench, too, since she wasn't distracted by the presence of a handsome man interested in her. *He is so talented,* she realized. The detail on the back of the bench reminded her of other wood-burning work she'd seen recently. She remembered the wooden sign that displayed *The Wesley Estate* at the foot of the property's hill. Reflecting on the gorgeous wooden sign's details, she had a feeling he'd crafted that piece, as well.

Noting the page number where she'd found the photo, she placed the picture on the nightstand to give to Phil tomorrow. She didn't want to risk damaging the photo by pressing it back between the pages. He probably didn't even know it was stowed away up here among Matthew's possessions, and she was certain he would cherish it. Then, she plopped back into bed, flipped to the front of the book, and started reading.

Not even a full page into the book, she lost herself in thought once more. *How strong can the foundation of a relationship between an Adamos and Wesley be?* she wondered. *We come from such different backgrounds. Our families, and countries, have such different ideals.* She wondered what her parents would say about her interest in a man that should have been a major client. Instead, she was his house guest, helping him sabotage her family's potential financial gains. She worried they would judge his age, too, even though he was only six years younger than her.

Then, she remembered what she had said to Phillip when he asked about her parents' opinion concerning her involvement with his land. *"Heck, let my family cut me out of the inheritance for all I care,"* she'd claimed. *"I don't want their dirty money."* As she reflected on the words that had poured out of her soul, she realized how true the sentiment was. Just as she had always forged her own path in life, including her own realty business, she knew she could accept choosing a path that diverged from the Adamos inheritance.

What was more, she could stomach disappointing her parents before she could stomach disappointing herself and all she stood for. Mother Nature was not a force to trifle with on this polluted, infested, combed-over Earth, and Anna respected every environment. Not to mention she held special awe for this environment, a biome unlike any other she'd seen in her world travels. *You sound like a Unimona Party sympathizer,* she thought to herself. *And so what if I do?*

Though she and Phillip had never labeled his political opinions aloud, she knew how he felt. She had always fancied herself skilled with reading between the lines of conversation, and she felt confident she understood his stance. A stance she could get behind. A stance she *was* getting behind. After all her research, discussions, and considerations concerning these current events, she had come upon her mid-life enlightenment. She knew for certain she believed in the core values of the Union for Mother Nature Party. *Let the chips fall where they may,* she thought.

After reading for a short while, Anna fell asleep with the book in her hands.

Chapter 19

The Rookie

PHILLIP COULDN'T SEEM to stop thinking about kissing Anna. All through breakfast, he watched her lips as she took sips of coffee or nibbled at her shakshuka on toast. He looked away every time he found himself at it again, and he hoped that Anna never picked up on his behavior. If she had picked up on his staring, which she likely had with how obviously he thought he was behaving, he hoped that she wouldn't feel uncomfortable about it. To him, the situation was getting to the point where he wasn't sure if he should openly say something about it to make sure he wasn't crossing any lines. He was well aware that they had shared multiple kisses and intimate moments yesterday, but he knew, too, that she had asked for space. For time. Now, he wasn't certain if he should be the one to bring up their relationship (if they were indeed in a relationship) or if he should wait for her move.

God, Matt would never let something like this situation go unspoken about if he was still alive to see it. He'd say some dumb crap about his baby brother falling in love. He'd make it into a catchphrase, something idiotic like, "My little twerp is twitterpated!" Just like all their inside jokes, the new saying would never die. A poignant, comforting thought struck him then: *As long as I remember him, Matthew's presence, his influence in my life, doesn't die either.*

Phillip found himself smiling at the thought. Somehow, the thought of his dead brother teasing the ever-loving crud out of him wasn't wholly depressing. Normally, the very idea of Matthew not being on earth to do something like that would have him reaching for the whiskey already, but not this time. The idea was still bittersweet, but the pain had lost its cutting edge for the moment.

Besides, Phillip knew that if Matthew were around to meet Anna, he'd absolutely love her. He almost heard his brother's voice saying, "She's a firecracker, that one. Hurricane in human skin, and twice as beautiful."

"What are you thinking about?"

Phillip started in his seat, turning to face Anna. "Huh?"

"I asked what you were thinking about. You were smiling."

"Oh," Phillip tried to rub away the blush he could feel crawling up the back of his neck. "Not much, just thinking about my brother."

"Oh, was it a happy memory, then?"

"More like what he would think of you," Phillip watched her out of the corner of his eye as she blushed and made a small noise of surprise. "I just think he'd like you. Want to get to know you, y'know?"

"I'm … I'm happy to hear that," Anna's face was as red as the peppers in their breakfast, and she was speaking to her lap, but he caught the flash of her smile, so he hoped he'd said something right.

They each turned their attention back to their food and let the moment pass naturally. Phillip tried desperately to remember their conversation last night and the priorities they had settled on tackling today. The two of them had something close to a lightning storm between them, but saving the land had to come first.

"So, I was thinking—"

"Phillip, where do—"

They both started speaking at the same time and stopped, each looking at the other in chagrin before he gestured to Anna to start.

"I was going to ask where you thought the best place to start on all this was," she explained. "When I spoke to the paralegal, it seemed simple enough, but we didn't look at the actual documentation, so I was thinking we might pull it up online and see what sorts of things we'll need to put together."

"That's not a bad idea," Phillip agreed readily. "I'll grab my laptop, and we can start a list."

Approaching the stairs and taking them with quick strides, he ventured to his room. Though he would rather spend the morning whiling away time in her arms, he was grateful for her prompt to action. Even though he felt like she would disappear in a puff of smoke, Anna clearly, wasn't going anywhere. She had made her stance and her willingness to help evident. They could discuss what their relationship would or could look like later.

After finding his laptop on his nightstand, he headed back downstairs to the dining room. He was happy to follow her lead on all these matters since she was knowledgeable about real estate. She was the one who had gathered intel from Rand's office to use against the slimy, capitalistic pig. And damn, did her initiative make him admire her even more. This woman, here with him as he embarked on a new journey, was like no one else on the planet. He could think of no one better and more formidable than her to help him overcome this mountain-sized obstacle. Truth be told, he could picture her at his side for the long haul. No matter if they had met a short time ago, he already knew with crystal clarity how he felt about her. She had proven her compassion and passion at every turn, despite their trials, even against one another.

At the foot of the stairs, he mentally shook himself. As loath as he was to do it, he knew he had to set aside these quickly blossoming feelings for Anna for the time being. Obviously, based on the fact that she had expressed an interest in jumping right to work, she was willing to help focus their priorities. As she said yesterday, he had to get his head in the game. He knew he needed her kind push to prioritize what needed to come first: his family's legacy.

⎯⚊⊸⫘⊶⚊⎯

Three hours later, Anna's head was buried in her arms, where she slumped over the dining room table, and Phillip was trying very hard not to snap a second pencil in frustration.

"How is this comprehensible to anyone?" he fumed. "It's like doing taxes, only there are no numbers, and they keep changing the definitions of the words."

"I'm so sorry, Phillip," Anna said, her voice muffled but clearly distressed. "When I spoke to the paralegal about it, she made it seem like it'd be so simple! I didn't think it would be this bad."

"Friggin' lawyers, I swear. It probably is comprehensible to her because she took lessons in how to speak demonese or something. That's what they learn in law school, isn't it? How to summon the devil and trick people into selling their souls?"

Anna sat up with a tight chuckle, rubbing her hands over her face.

"It must be," she replied, finally looking over at him. "I don't know how anyone could figure this out unless they had some sort of all-knowing being helping them."

"No, no, I doubt she summoned anything to help her with something as simple as this," Phillip joked, turning away from the opened computer screen. "Obviously, most of the summoning happens in graduate school."

"Oh, of course!" Anna's eyes were dancing now, her misery starting to fall away. "So, she would already know these sorts of things. But don't you think they'd have some sort of familiar around, then? An animal or an imp, perhaps?"

"Of course!" Phillip exclaimed. "Not an imp, though. It'd have to be an ogre."

"Oh? And why is that?"

"I've met him."

"Have you?" Anna was openly laughing now. "What's his name then?"

"Mark."

Anna's answering laughter held too many snorts to be considered ladylike, and so far, it was Phillip's favorite he'd heard from her.

They spent a bit more time marking the similarities between Anna's family friend and the beast of legend, but they were soon interrupted by the sound of the doorbell. They shared a confused glance before Phillip got up, Anna trailing after him as he walked to the door.

He knew it was stupid to be anxious just because someone was at the door. It wasn't like he and Anna had announced to the world what their plans were. There was no flag of subterfuge flying over his house or whatever. So then, why did he feel tension winding through his arms and shoulders? He could tell Anna felt it as well. Her footsteps were silent behind him, carrying her with a cat's hunting grace.

They reached the door just as a second ring sounded. Phillip could just make out the dark figure of the person on the other side through the frosted glass panes set into the middle of the door.

Reaching out a hand, he felt Anna slip to his other side, just behind the door, to listen without being immediately noticeable in the dark interior of the house. Philip grabbed the handle and opened the door as smoothly as possible, trying not to give the stranger any indication of his tension.

When he finally laid eyes on his visitor, he couldn't help but feel stupid for all the useless buildup. At his door was a man he'd never seen before. The man was of middling height and build and looked maybe in his mid-to-late twenties. He had artfully styled, floppy brown hair and large eyes so dark it looked like they were all pupils.

Phillip waved a hand behind the door to let Anna know it wasn't anything serious and leaned his shoulder against the door frame. "Yeah?" he asked, not unkindly.

"Are you Phillip Wesley?" the man asked in a mellow voice.

"Depends. What do you need him for?"

The man's mouth twisted, but Phillip couldn't tell if it was in displeasure or to hide a smile. "I'm trying to get in touch with Anna Adamos, and I believe you might be able to help me."

"I might," Phillip hedged. "But it'd probably be easier to look her up online and reach out through more formal means. Have you tried calling Adamos Realty?"

"I'm afraid I don't have the time to handle all the red tape that going through official channels would require. I'm also afraid I'll need a better level of discretion than that approach would offer," his reply was brisk, but Phillip got the impression this dude was getting anxious. "I understand you might be in regular contact with her as you're going through the process of selling your land?"

"Look, dude," Phillip interrupted, suddenly tired of playing some kind of beat-around-the-bush game. "I don't know you, and you haven't even introduced yourself or told me why you want to speak to Anna. I'm afraid you'll have to give me a little more than that if you want anything from me."

The man's brows knit, and he considered for a moment before nodding. "Apologies for not introducing myself. I'm afraid I'm a tad frazzled at the moment. My name is Talmadge Clark. I can tell you a little more about why I'm here, but I'd rather do it inside if that's okay with you?"

Phillip caught movement out of the corner of his eye as Anna slipped farther into the shadows. He opened the door wider and stepped to the side, allowing Talmadge room to step into the house. The man seemed hesitant to do so at first but took a visible breath and stepped in with the air of a man taking a plunge.

Phillip led the way to the armchairs around the fireplace, and the two men settled without any further niceties. The host gestured for Talmadge to take the chair facing the windows, so the man's back was to Anna's hiding spot.

"So, why do you need to speak to Anna so badly, and secretly, at that?"

Talmadge seemed to search for words for a moment before he said, "I have information about a ... *contact* that she and I share. It's of a sensitive nature, and I'm putting myself at great risk trying to bring it forward. I believe Anna can help me get the protection I need when I do so."

"Who's this contact?"

"I'm afraid I can't share that."

"And what makes you believe Anna's in any position to help you? She's not exactly a linebacker."

"That's not the protection I'll be needing. I'm afraid bringing this forward will ruin me here. I need someone with contacts to help a man disappear and rebuild his life as someone else. Anna runs in the right circles to put me in immediate contact with these people."

Phillip was about to continue his questioning, still not satisfied with the answers he was getting, but Anna stopped him by stepping out of the shadows by the door. Talmadge saw his distraction and turned to follow his eye line, startling out of his chair when he saw Anna crossing the room.

"Miss Adamos! Well, this is fortuitous!"

"You said your name is Talmadge Clark?" she asked, extending her hand for him to shake. "I don't believe we've met."

"It is, and we haven't," he said, quickly grasping her hand.

"Then, tell me how you know so much about me and why you think you need my help."

Talmadge eyed Phillip suspiciously, but Anna only raised her brow and waited.

"I work for the Stardade Federal Government," the man started. "When the revolution was starting up, I met a man named Mark Rand while attending a conference for students interested in government work …."

As he continued to tell it, Talmadge's story was absolutely wild. Somehow, he'd been put in some sort of government secretarial position from the start and risen through the ranks in similar supportive roles. Due to his role, he'd been able to collect evidence of some sort of wealthy cabal that'd had the previous president assassinated. That group had tweaked the last election to get a puppet president in power. Talmadge had had the information for a time and hadn't known what to do with it. He'd heard Mark speak about a family friend named Anna, and something in the way he spoke made Talmadge decide to look her up. The more he'd found, the more he'd hoped she could help him.

At one point, Anna asked him why he was willing to nuke his own life just to bring this information to light.

"Miss Adamos," Talmadge said, a hard glint in his eyes. "Part of the reason Mr. Rand chose to help me was that I am in a position he can easily manipulate. I was raised in a low-class family and had to work three times as hard to make any social connections. Networking is the lifeblood of politics, and I was playing with a severe handicap. He knew he could use that fact to his advantage and make a good worker bee out of me. However, he miscalculated. Mr. Rand seems to have forgotten that, sometimes, a person becomes a civil servant because they truly believe in their country. My people are not perfect, but I will do everything I can to protect them from snakes like Rand. I will see my life's work burn before I allow that man to do any more harm to Stardade."

"Well …" Anna sat back. Her eyes took on a dangerous, hopeful shine. "It looks like we might be able to help each other out, Mr. Clark."

Chapter 20

The Cake

THE TRIO SAT around the laptop, Talmadge at the helm, problem-solving with Anna as Phillip kept track of actions they needed to take and documents they needed to collect. They had moved the laptop to the living room to make use of the extra space, but the chairs hadn't been especially useful with three of them and such a small laptop screen. Eventually, they had all given up and ended up in a little huddle sitting on the ground with the laptop in a place of honor on the coffee table. The backdrop of their adventure was the Wesley Estate vista.

Talmadge was in the middle of explaining how they might be able to expedite the whole process of memorializing the land by using one of his contacts. Then, their work was interrupted again by the sound of the doorbell.

Phillip and Anna caught their eyes and shared wry looks. Phillip was about to comment about his growing popularity when the distinct sound of a key in the lock made him freeze.

"Philly!" Jaq's voice trumpeted from the entryway. "I'm here to apologize for being the worst friend ever! Really, I recognize how sh—Oh, hello …" she cut herself off as she spotted them clustered together on the floor like a bunch of middle schoolers. She held a clear container of pink, frosted cake.

"Jaq, hey!" Phillip scrambled to his feet, trying desperately to act casual. Based on Jaq's expression, he'd achieved the opposite effect. "I wasn't expecting you! Anna and her friend were just stopping by about, um, about the land …."

Jaq just looked at him, eyes intent. "The land," she said. "The land you were solidly decided on *not* selling? That land?"

"Ye—um, yep. Yep, that land." Phillip felt his hand go to the back of his neck as his best friend of more than a decade just kept staring at him.

"Is that cake?" he heard Anna ask from behind him.

"Looks like strawberry," Talmadge chimed in, walking forward and noting the fruit perched atop the dessert. "Allow me to introduce myself. I am Talmadge Clark, Secretary of Commerce to the Stardade President's Cabinet." He held out his hand, but hers were full of cake and keys.

"Oh, wow. That's a mouthful," Jaq said, blushing. "I'm Jaqueline Fox. But my friends call me Jaq." As Phillip took the cake from her, she added, "Are you friends with the secretary of state, Phillip?"

"Um, yeah, sure," Phillip said, his hands feeling awkward as he held the cake.

"Jaqueline Fox is a beautiful name," Talmadge said. "It suits you."

"Thank you." Her blush deepened.

"And I'm Anna Adamos," she said as she approached. "Nice to meet you, Jaq." Anna bypassed the formalities and went in for a hug, which made Jaq bristle. "How long have you and Phil been friends?"

"Phil?" Jaq asked, tasting the nickname and pursing her lips as it soured. "*Philly* and I go way back. Why are you here?" She turned towards her friend. "Why is she here? I thought you weren't selling your land."

Phillip started to say, "I'm not—"

"And why is—I'm sorry, Talmadge was it—here?" Jaq asked, throwing her hands into the air so that her keys jingled. "What's going on?"

"Here, let's go into the kitchen to cut the cake," Phillip said. "I'll explain."

"If it's all the same to you," Talmadge said, "I'd like to be present for this discussion. Explain my own situation. I can't be too careful with how this information trickles."

"I meant to discuss *my* land," Phillip said with a shrug, "but feel free to give your spiel, too. That decision is yours. Jaq has been my friend forever. She's trustworthy. I'll vouch for her."

"If I may say so," Talmadge said, pausing to clear his throat, "with a friend as lovely as this fine lady, you appear to keep good company."

Jaq, who had clearly caught the government official's attention, giggled. "You're quite the sweet talker."

"May I shake your hand now, Miss Jaqueline Fox?"

"Please," she said, holding out her pink fingernails, "call me Jaq."

"Seems we've become fast friends," he said, shaking her hand as they made steady eye contact.

Phillip and Anna exchanged a smirk.

"It seems you've saved the day," Phillip said. "I just realized I've been an awful host, not offering refreshments to my company. Jaq, can you help me cut this cake?"

"Sure," Jaq said, hesitating to follow him to the kitchen.

"Talmadge, what can I get you to drink?"

"Water for me, please."

"I'll make tea, too," Phillip said over his shoulder, "Sound good, Anna?"

"Perfect!"

Once the two were alone in the kitchen, Phillip set down the cake on the counter and turned to Jaq.

She waved daintily over her shoulder as she walked into the room.

Phillip put his fists on his hips and raised his eyebrows. He lowered his voice to say, "It would seem that Secretary of Commerce Talmadge Clark has a *thing* for you."

"Do you think so?" she lowered her voice and tucked a strand of ginger hair behind her ear.

He nodded. "He caught your eye, didn't he?"

"Was I *that* obvious?" she fiddled with the end of a strand of hair.

"Only to someone who has known you for as long as I have."

"Wait, don't try to distract me." She crossed her arms. "What is this secret meeting all about?"

"Go grab the cake cutter and plates," he said, putting the tea kettle on the stove, "and I'll explain every—well, I'll explain what I can." He turned on the gas and flicked the flame to life. "Honestly, we could use your insight on the financials of the whole ordeal."

"You know I'm always happy to lend a hand where accounting is concerned." As familiar with this kitchen as her own, she walked directly to pull the items he requested. "But what's Talmadge's deal?"

"Talmadge's story is both complicated and his to tell."

"I see." She set the utensil and plates next to the cake. "How can I help?"

⬦

Over tea and cake, Talmadge spilled his guts to Jaq, in the same manner, he had to Phillip and Anna mere hours ago. Upon this telling, though, Phillip noticed Talmadge painted himself in a better light, more a victim than a perpetrator. Sure, during the initial confession, he had explained his involvement in a way that divulged his ignorant participation, but this time he seemed even more apologetic. Phillip suspected the government man's enthrallment with his childhood friend had something to do with his choice of words.

Shortly after the speech's start, Phillip abandoned his plate of cake. He hoped he appeared distracted from the dessert rather than disgusted with it. In fact, they had all done their best to spare Jaq's feelings by complimenting the hard, dry cake upon each of their first (and only) bites. Phillip appreciated his friend's gesture, and he would die before he'd tell her she couldn't bake to save her life.

"Since you are a trusted associate of Mr. Wesley and Miss Adamos," Talmadge finished his monologue, "I feel that you could be an asset to the small, trusted circle we've built here. What are your skills?"

"I am the CPA for a small accounting firm—actually the *only* accounting firm—on the island."

"Fascinating," Talmadge said, leaning forward. "Tell me more about that."

"The Fox Financial Firm handles the taxes, investments, and retirement accounts for all registered companies in the historic district and the Starlight Inn."

Phillip realized that Talmadge had just triggered her favorite topic. *This discussion could take a while,* he realized. "We can't fill up on cake alone," the host said, hoping Jaq didn't see through his charade to dispose of his cake and avoid money talk. "Let me see what I can whip up."

"I'll help," Anna said, picking up her cake-laden plate and following him into the kitchen.

"In addition to our business-to-business avenues," continued Jaq after dismissing them with a wave, "we work with a dozen remote clients on the mainland …."

Chapter 21

The AID

ONCE THE TWO were alone, Phillip dumped his slice of cake in the trash can. "Oops," he said without meaning it. "The two people enthralled with one another are alone."

"Do you mean them or us?" she said, bumping her hip into his as she ditched her own cake on top of his in the trash.

"Yes."

He took Anna's plate, stacked it on his, and set the dirty dishes on the counter. Placing his hands on her hips, he felt delighted when her hands went to his shoulders to wrap around his neck. Her body pressed close to his. She looked into his eyes. When he leaned down to kiss her adorable lips, her eyes fluttered closed as she sighed. Closing his own eyes, his hands explored, tightening around her.

Way too soon, she pulled back.

"I'd love to continue, but I'm starving. What are we making for dinner?"

"Um." He leaned back, still holding Anna close, to peek in the nearby pantry. "Lemme check."

She leaned her head against his chest to look with him, and his heart fluttered.

He lost his train of thought, wondering instead if she could hear his heartbeat quicken. *She smells like honey,* he thought. *I could hold her all day.*

"Status report," she prompted.

"Ah, hmm. Unfortunately, I don't think we have any dinner food."

As she examined the pantry, he realized after he spoke that he had easily included her in his use of the word *we*. Feeling as though what's his was hers, even at these early stages of their relationship, he could picture them sharing this home together. An image of them sharing coffee and watching dawn through the back windows flashed through his mind, warming his soul.

"Did you not notice the spaghetti and tomato sauce?" she asked, pulling him from his fantasy.

"The what now?"

"Right here." She let him go and stepped in front of him to bend down. Her backside brushed against him, and he felt his cheeks heat up. "You have an unopened box and jar." From the bottom shelf, she pulled the items and showed him. "Let's make this. Where's your spice cabinet?"

"I forgot that was even in there." He scratched the back of his head. "Check the expiration date. They are probably emergency supplies my mom bought when the war started."

She examined the supplies. "They're good until the end of this year."

"Oh, nice. Can I be honest with you?"

"Always." With her hands still holding the food, the pasta rattled as she hugged his waist.

He took a deep breath as he internally grasped for his dissipating thought. "I don't know how to cook spaghetti."

"Don't know h—" She stepped back. "Where do you keep your pot and colander because you are learning right now, Mr. Wesley."

"Um. What's a colander?"

"What's—? You're lucky you're so handsome." She set the supplies on the counter. "And lucky I'm so resourceful."

They shared a laugh at his expense. Then, they got to work.

Phillip came to admire just how resourceful Anna Adamos was. He adored the way she bossed him around the kitchen like he was some hopeless sous chef on his first day. His favorite moment of the experience happened when she dipped the wooden spoon into the bowl of red sauce and held it out for him to taste. When they met eyes, he could see the twinkle of excitement in hers. After he tasted the exquisite yet simple sauce with hints of garlic, thyme, and rosemary, he tasted it once more on her lips.

"Let's plate the food," she whispered against his lips. "In a minute."

They shared a slow, deep kiss.

"Divvy up the pasta, my darling."

"Mhm."

She gave him one more tender smooch, then scootched the spoon between their lips before pushing his face back a tad. "Dinner time."

"As you wish." He pulled out four plates and readied the meals.

"My turn." She poured the steaming sauce on the pasta.

"How did you do that?" he asked.

"I just heated the sauce in the microwave," she said without looking up, "which you honestly need to clean because that thing is *nasty*."

"No." He chuckled and scratched his head. "How did you essentially make dinner for four out of thin air? When I looked in that pantry, I just saw chips and peanuts."

She used a towel to wipe the sauce off the edge of one plate like a professional chef. "I like to call it the Analytical Investigator Deviation."

"The *What Now* Deviation? Did you make that up?"

"Sure did." Wiping her hands on the towel, she admired their handiwork. "The Analytical Investigator Deviation, or AID for short," she said, her brown eyes lighting up, "is when someone has the ability to step back and investigate a situation to analyze it from a different perspective. Thus, their thought pattern appears as a deviation because it's different."

"Huh." He felt the smile gracing his lips and realized he could listen to her share intellectual ideas all night.

"The same thought pattern shows up when, for example, someone comes up with an idea in a boardroom that blows the other ideas out of the water."

"Ah, I think I get it. Like when a brainstorm has a lightning strike."

"Oooh, I like that." Her smile lit up the whole room.

"Ready to feed the crew?" He picked up two plates.

"First, while we're still alone, can I just express something I need?"

"Of course, darling." He set the plates back down.

"I want to go on a date with you more than I could probably ever express. I want to do the whole dating ordeal, you know? Like be your girlfriend and go to dinner and all that feel-good stuff …."

"But?"

She sighed. "But I need us to wait until we finish this paperwork and whole clandestine scheme before we dive into our new relationship. I want to do this thing right."

He hugged her around the waist, loving how her hands felt as they wrapped around his neck. Kissing her forehead, he relished the moment that would be over too soon. He leaned back and looked down into her gorgeous eyes. "Deal."

"Thanks, hon."

"Always." He kissed her forehead once more.

"Is that your dinner bell?" she asked, pointing at the old, tin-and-copper bell. "Can I ring it?"

He observed the dusty thing, which his father had hung just inside the kitchen entryway nearly two decades ago. *When was the last time I even thought about that bell?* he wondered, feeling a pang of upset at forgetting his family's traditions. He guessed this forgotten memento's use was one side effect of living alone. "Dad used to ring it every single night."

"Really?" She looked reverent at the symbol of his memories.

"Yeah, we could hear it from the garden, believe it or not. But it hasn't been rung in," he huffed out a breath as he thought, "at least a year. Be my guest." He nodded towards the bell.

With fervor, she clanged it louder than his youngest brother, Ethan, ever did, which was saying something considering he was the loudest bell ringer in the house. As dust flew off the object, the clanging dusted some cobwebs off his heart, too. Her glee made him smile from the inside out.

"That was fun." She giggled and grabbed the other two plates to place on the table.

"Fun suits you."

"Thank you kindly," she said, blushing a beautiful pink. "Do you happen to have a dry, red wine? It would pair so well with the flavor profile we crafted."

He set down the plates, then peered into the wine closet adjacent to the pantry. Opening the door, he reflected on the sauce's taste and considered several options. "How's Chianti?"

"Perfect, Phil! Don't forget the glasses."

His heart sped up once more as he followed her instructions. She had used the simple nickname he had loved from the moment she first uttered it. No one had ever called him Phil before. On the island, everyone, from family to teachers, from friends to acquaintances, just used the full version. *Well, except for Jaq,* he realized, *but Philly sounds silly.*

When everyone filled the empty chairs and the empty table, Phillip raised his glass of wine. "To preserving the land."

"To preserving the land," they echoed, raising their glasses to clink together.

"I have a good feeling about Operation Save the Heart of Astiri," Anna said.

Every member of the team agreed before tucking into their modest meal.

Chapter 22

The Flowers

PHILLIP VERY CAREFULLY stopped thinking as he rumbled at a stoplight on one of the main avenues in the bowels of Prijipati. This brain-halting action was on repeat, as he kept forgetting he was trying not to consider all of the issues with what he'd chosen to do with his weekend. The problem was that he kept getting distracted by how *beautiful* the city was.

There should be some rule that declares any country subjugating its neighbors is required to look gross and bleak, and like the evil lair in a children's cartoon, Phillip thought as he pulled his eyes away from a glimmering, colorful storefront. Somehow, he had been walking around his whole life with an image in his head of Valtross like some dystopian hovel. Despite the pictures he'd seen, he'd imagined it all smoke-smeared and grimy à la Castle Grayskull. Now, confronted with its, quite literally, awesome architecture and dazzling skyline, the dissonance made him feel a little dizzy.

The border crossing Phillip had chosen was located at one end of a bridge spanning the length of a bay. While cresting the peak of the said bridge at a crawl in the long line down to the crossing, he'd been able to watch Prijipati's skyscrapers populate the horizon until the shining glass and steel mountains glittered in all their grandeur down the line of the bay and spilled over the gentle arch of the coast, overlooking the ocean.

He'd expected the initial amazement. Any city was stunning, given the distance. But he had also expected it to fade into grim disappointment as he drew nearer and, eventually, entered the city proper.

No such thing had happened.

Apparently, Valtross found it acceptable to pollute its neighbor's and business partner's land but found doing the same to its own abhorrent. He'd left the glittering blue bay behind to wind his way through streets lined with shady palm trees and buildings bursting with greenery. Birds flitted between the buildings, and squirrels and dassies competed for the best territory on the ground.

He noticed a few pedestrians giving him cold looks while he idled at stop lights, and his first thought was that they recognized him as a Valtrossian and looked down on him in some xenophobic, classist rage. Finally, after catching the same look from an old woman tottering across the street in front of him, he finally realized that the people he'd passed were glaring at his *truck*, not him. They *disapproved of him, but it had more to do with the fact that his junker was powered by fossil fuels*, not his country of origin.

Still classist, he thought, obstinate even in the face of being proven paranoid.

When he finally passed a sheet fountain that drizzled its water down a two-story rock face resembling the cliffs in his much-loved valley, Phillip finally admitted defeat. He came to rest at a stop sign and rolled down his window to listen to the mix of city, wildlife, and water. Pausing a moment, Phillip closed his eyes, breathed the hot, green city air into his lungs, and admitted to himself that Anna's country was gorgeous. Their foreign policy left much to be desired, but it couldn't be all bad if Valtross housed a city like this.

Really, after seeing everything around him, it would have surprised him more if Anna *didn't* have an interest in architecture.

A harsh beeping startled him out of his moment of peace, and he immediately took his foot off the brake and started forward, waving to the person stopped behind him. He was close enough to his destination. He should find a place to park.

⊸⧲⊸

Twenty minutes later, Phillip was standing at the door to an apartment with a bouquet of dusky pink roses, and purple lilacs gripped in sweaty hands. The petals looked strangely like velvet in the blue-white light of the hallway. The apartment building had been fancy, with a smooth stone exterior and a high, solid wall surrounding the entire estate.

Phillip had been nervous about how he'd get in, but he helped hold the door open for a woman whose literal hands were full of groceries and metaphorical hands were full of twin girls each pulling at her skirt. She buzzed, he pulled, and the doorman took one look at his flowers and let him go.

Phillip took a deep breath and raised his hand, forcing himself to knock before he could talk himself out of it.

"Just a second!" Anna's voice rang through the wood of the door. Not a moment later, she swung it inward, releasing a breeze that smelled like her perfume and the stew she must be simmering on the stove.

"Phil!" She exclaimed with surprise and delight. Then, again, with slightly less delight and more astonishment, *"Phil?!"*

Phillip held out the flowers and laughed a little self-consciously, "Surprise? I hope I didn't come at a bad time …."

"No! No, please come in," Anna hastily opened her door wider and stepped aside to make room. "Sorry, I was just surprised to see you here. You know … in Valtross?"

"It is a bit like worlds colliding, isn't it?" he said as he stepped in and shamelessly looked around. The apartment was all high ceilings and clean lines. He wasn't sure if Anna had hired an interior decorator or if she'd done it herself, but either way, the decorations danced beautifully along a line between elegant and comfortable. Across the apartment, the opposite wall housed large windows and a set of sliding glass doors leading out to a balcony. He was too far back to get a good look at her view, but if his memory of his walk over and sense of direction served him well, it looked out on a quiet city street and corner park.

"I can see why you were so charmed by my place," he said wryly. "You practically live under a rock."

"You can never have too much beauty in your life. And don't even start with me, I've seen your valley, and this doesn't hold a candle," she said, her voice just as dry. "Now, if you're done being a butthead, are those for me?"

"Oh, yes." He held out the flowers again, and Anna took them.

"They're beautiful! Thank you." She blushed, burying her face in the bouquet for a moment before bustling over to snag an empty vase from a sideboard. "Follow me to the kitchen? I could use your help filling the vase."

Phil complied and dutifully stuck the vase under the faucet as he watched Anna stir the stew and turn to the flowers. She fetched a pair of scissors and started snipping the stems of the flowers, setting them aside in a separate pile.

"It really is lovely to see you," she said, eyes focused on her task but voice shy. "I didn't expect you to want to come to Valtross."

"Well, I didn't," Phil said, "but I wanted to see you more than I didn't want to come if that makes any sense."

Anna looked up, her eyes sparkling. "It does," she whispered. The light streaming in from the windows made her eyes and hair glow golden, and Phillip found he couldn't look away. Her chipmunk cheeks made her eyes squint as she smiled and said, "Phil, you're gonna overflow."

Phillip blinked back to himself and down at what he was doing. "I'm gonna—? I'm gonna overflow!" He was quick in shutting off the water but still had to pour some back into the sink. Embarrassed, he handed the full vase to Anna and watched her arrange the bouquet to her liking.

"So you're cooking stew for dinner?"

"Hm? Oh, yeah. It's nothing special, just some left-over odds and ends that needed to be eaten. You're welcome to join unless you have other plans."

"I was actually hoping I might be able to take you out?" He asked for his shoes, feeling his neck heat.

Anna sat up straight and turned to look at him.

"Out? Like, on a date?"

Phillip felt a smile quirk on his lips but still didn't look up as he nodded.

"Like, the thing we agreed not to do until your land was safe?"

He nodded again.

"Does this mean?"

Phillip finally looked up, his mouth split in a wide grin. "I gave the last of the documents to Talmadge yesterday. It's technically not safe yet, but at this point, we've done all we can, so I figured it counted."

Anna's answering smile was just as brilliant as his. "Oh, it definitely counts," she agreed. "Forget the stew. I'll save it for another day. We're going out!"

Walking hand-in-hand, the lovebirds traversed the bustling sidewalks of the capital city. The place was only more dazzling, shared with his date's incredible company. Storefronts, which varied in purpose from coffee to clothing shops, lined either side of the street. Though he hoped to appear to wander aimlessly, Phillip subtly steered them in the direction of his evening plans. He was hoping to add a layer of intrigue by surprising Anna.

"So," he cleared his throat, "I did some research on reviews for restaurants in the area ..." He hesitated, buying some time as they approached the venue.

"Mhm?" she hummed, giant, brown eyes glued to his warming face.

"And I was wondering what you think ..." He paused for his best rendition of dramatic effect.

"Go on."

"Of ..." He let go of her hand to turn her towards the restaurant at their side. "Ta-da!"

"The Twilight Palace?" she squeaked, bouncing on the balls of her feet. "Did you get a reservation? This place packs out every Friday night."

"I sure did." He flashed a proud smile, glad he'd planned ahead.

"But wait, when did you do that?"

"Mind your business, Miss Adamos." He put his fists on his hips.

"Had you already called ahead before you got to my place?"

"Maybe," he sang.

"So, you knew I'd say yes to a date with you."

"I was hopeful."

She looped her arm through his. "Good!"

He opened the door for her and said to the hostess, "I have a reservation under Wesley."

"Ah, Mr. Wesley. Welcome to The Twilight Palace, both of you. I have a table for two on the balcony."

"That's correct."

"Right this way." The hostess pulled a couple of menus and led them up the stairs.

"On the balcony?" Anna whispered with a thrill.

"Only the best for a princess." Phillip winked.

"Eek!" She squeezed his arm. "I'm so excited. I'm choosing to ignore the sarcasm I heard in your voice."

"Excellent." He smirked at her. "My plan is working."

She swatted at his arm playfully with her hand.

They settled at the table on the private balcony overlooking the street, the coastline peaking between two skyscrapers. According to the reviews, outside of the beach itself, this locale was the best spot in the entire city to watch the sunset.

As part of their delightful conversation, they reminisced on how much their lives felt changed since they'd met. With drinks, the two shared a traditional, Valtrossian cuisine of stew from the same cauldron, which they served family-style into their own bowls.

"Is this the same kind of stew you were making this evening?" Phil asked.

"Sure, but I could never make one this good, even if I tried for a hundred years."

They laughed companionably.

"I have to say, this Valtrossian food does not disappoint."

"Of course, it doesn't. It's the food of *my* culture."

"I won't say that I'm falling for your culture, but I'm falling for you, so pretty close."

The words had fallen out of his mouth with no warning. He was so caught up in the banter, over which he was still chuckling, that he didn't realize at first that he had shown his hand. Then, he saw Anna's huge eyes above the spoonful of food frozen halfway to her face. She set down the uneaten bite and put her hands in her lap.

"What did you say?"

"Just that …" He scratched his neck. "I'm falling for you or something, I guess."

She giggled, and the tension fizzled out of him. "You oughta work on your proclamations, Phil." Her eyes twinkled with delight.

He forced a laugh. "Yeah, I know. So smooth. I'll do better next time."

She picked up her spoon and pointed it at him. "Promise?"

"Cross my heart."

"Good, because I'm falling for you, and I need to know where your head is at."

"You're—Really?" His body felt abuzz with electricity.

"Mhm." She nodded, a pink blush nearly imperceptible on her cheeks in the twilight.

Just in time for sunset, the two received dessert of a chocolate malva pudding for two. As the sun threaded the needle between the two glass-and-steel skyscrapers, orange rays reflected over the windows. The buildings lit up as though they were aflame, sending sparkles of glowing light over the city goers and their surroundings. Beyond the cityscape, the sun melted into the horizon, sending flaming starlight dancing over the ocean waves and sugar sand. On a crosswalk perfectly aligned with the couple's vantage point, pedestrians paused in the street to watch the sunset. The cars on either side of them halted but did not honk. The glorious, cosmic display enraptured everyone. And Anna and Phillip had the best seats in the house.

Wordlessly, she reached across the table and took his hands in her soft grip. Above her radiant smile, tears glistened like sunstones in her eyes. When she started to cry, Phillip reached across the table and wiped the tears from her cheeks.

"Thank you for showing me part of all the beauty this world has to offer," she said.

Chapter 23

The Scheme

1 Month Later

ANNA HAD EXPECTED the process of transporting a federal official across his country's border to cause a fuss. But the border patrol officer waved her through after only checking her identification with Talmadge as her anonymous passenger. She wasn't sure if the guard had recognized her.

When the group was planning the departure, they had considered sending Talmadge and her in Phillip's car so hers wouldn't be recognizable. They had nixed the idea when she pointed out his giant, red truck—which took gas unlike most Valtrossian cars—would stand out like a sore thumb. She reminded herself, too, that an Adamos crossing the border, especially one who had business in Stardade, was a common occurrence.

On the other hand, she doubted that any of the patrol officers recognized Talmadge, an obscure cabinet member (no offense to his status). The two professionals crossing into Valtross, which business people were wont to do at this locale, apparently didn't raise any eyebrows.

After a month of careful preparation, scheming, and data-gathering in the name of Operation Save the Wesley Land, Anna realized she was on edge. After all, they were on their way to the soon-to-be fugitive's classified safehouse. Anna and her passenger were the only two who knew his final destination. Talmadge needed safety from the cabal that he sought to take down. Once Team Wesley knew the facts about the assassination of Stardade's former president, they weren't willing to take any risks.

Talmadge had brought the bare essentials for survival and planning in a duffel bag, leaving even his cell phone and laptop back at his home. Instead, he carried an external hard drive full of digitized files. He planned to spend his time at the secluded location organizing and processing this information on his own, using one of the Wesley brother's old laptops.

Once the two were in Valtross, Anna purchased a burner phone with cash from a busy gas station. When she turned around to exit, she saw none other than Mark Rand standing behind her.

"Fancy meeting you here, Anna," he said, sounding for all the world like a villain in a children's movie.

Thank God Talmadge is in the car, she thought. *I pray he kept up his hood, so Mark didn't see him.* Doing her best to act nonchalant, she said, "Yes, Mark. What a coincidence! What are you doing here?"

He held up his cup and pointed to the coffee shop at the next counter over. "Stardade never managed to franchise any Starbucks locations." He emitted a condescending chuckle. "Just stopped on my way back into Valtross for some *real* coffee. Unfortunately, my offices on the other side of the border can barely function without my bi-weekly presence." He chuckled again.

He must think he's so clever. She thought as she forced a giggle. *Gross.*

"And you?" He sipped his coffee and stared expectantly.

"What about me?" She eyed the door but didn't want to rush the conversation and raise his suspicion.

"What brings you to this particular locale? Your car doesn't take gas."

"Oh, I was—on business!"

"Speaking of …" he walked towards the door, which he opened for her. "After you."

She seized her opportunity to exit and hedge closer to her car. Looking to ensure Talmadge was hidden, which he was, she stood between Mark and her car. "Speaking of business?" she prompted.

"Are you here for me?" he asked.

"For you?"

She took a beat to look into his harsh eyes.

"Oh," she said, "for the property, yes. Yes, I am. I had to speak to Phil—lip Wesley about the land again. He really doesn't want to give up that plot."

"I was wondering what has been taking so long. Wasn't your initial meeting a month ago?"

"What can I say? The guy has a mind of his own."

"How … plebeian."

"Quite." Her voice fell flat on her own ears.

"Well, in any event, please update me by the end of the week. In fact, why don't we get together for dinner on Friday night to discuss the future."

"The future?"

"Yes, I have quite the plans for Rand Mining Corporation. Naturally, they involve you."

"Me?"

"Ohohoh! Leave the details to me, darling." He brushed his hand over her arm, making her force down a gag. "I'll send you a calendar invite."

"Sure, sure, I'll look for it." *The last thing I want to do is have dinner with that awful man,* she thought as she backed away, *but I need to behave like I normally would and get Talmadge out of here.*

"Goodbye, my fair Adamos."

"See ya around." She watched him walk away before diving into the driver's seat. *Thank God he didn't notice my car was still on. She* thought as she whispered to Talmadge through her teeth, "Keep your head down."

"I know," he said under his hoodie as Anna drove off. "I saw him. Do you think he saw me?"

"No, he would've said something if he had." They were back on the highway. "He might be a snake in the grass, but he isn't afraid to call out a suspicious situation. We have his misguided trust in me to work with."

"Why was he here?"

"Just a cup of coffee on his way out of Stardade. He goes to his offices there all the time. It wasn't out of the realm of likelihood that I'd run into him here. I should've chosen a gas station farther from the border."

"So, you don't think Rand has any idea what we've been working on, then?"

"No, I don't think he knows. But I'm going to have dinner with him this week. I can check out his plans. When we're one-on-one, he's surprisingly frank."

"At least we have that going for us."

"At least."

The two shared a relieved sigh to shake off their tension.

As Anna drove on her homeland's interstate, Talmadge set up his new phone. He wrote down only the number on a piece of paper, which he gave to her for safekeeping.

"Don't worry," she said, "I won't program this number into my phone, just like we discussed. Everyone's safety is our top priority. Thank you again for helping us file the necessary paperwork with the National Park System."

"Of course. Do you think, maybe, if it's okay," he said, "you could perhaps give this number to Jaq, too? Just in case, you know, she needs it? Silly of me, but I forgot to write down everyone's numbers. Jaq was so helpful and supportive during this whole ordeal. Oh, and I promised her I'd give her my family's recipe for rhubarb pie when I can."

"Sure thing, Talmadge." Anna felt the knowing smile sneak onto her lips. *He didn't ask me to give this number to Phillip*, she realized. *I knew it. He's interested in getting to know Jaqueline.*

When Anna dropped Talmadge at the motel outside of the capital's suburbs, he stood at her open car window.

"Remember to pay in cash," she said.

"Right. So weird in this century. Thank you for all that you've done, Miss Adamos. Will you thank Mr. Wesley for me?"

"I think that orchestrating a master plan as a group constitutes us all being on a first-name basis, don't you think?"

They shared a laugh, releasing more of their tension. His safety was almost assured at this secure location. They all just had to leave him alone to do his work and let the pieces fall into place.

"Want me to thank Jaq, too?" she asked.

"Mind if I do that myself?" his eyes glistened with hope.

"I'll call her to give her your number the moment I get home."

He sighed and tapped the inside of the window frame on her shoulder. "Thank you. Thank you, Anna."

"You're welcome. And thank *you* for your support in removing some red tape." When he nodded and started to walk away, she said softly, "Be safe, Talmadge."

Chapter 24

The Downfall

MARK TEXTED ANNA the details of their reservation as soon as she agreed to have dinner with him. He was a regular guest at L'étoile Du Nord, having the privilege of regular tennis matches with the owner at the country club they both attended. The restaurant was one of the best in Prijipati, and Mark never had a negative experience when he invited future business partners. He would almost say the establishment was a good luck charm if he believed in such banal forces.

Anna hadn't responded to his text, but he wasn't worried about it. She was a good girl, and they had a bright future together. He knew she had a solid head on her shoulders and wouldn't pass up such a good deal. Marrying him would execute so many benefits for her and her company's future.

The sun had set the skyline of Prijipati to glowing, and Mark observed the view from his regular table on the balcony of the little building. The restaurant's aesthetic was one of minimalist luxury. The chairs were all high-backed, padded white leather, and the tablecloths and napkins an indulgent shade of sea blue. It resonated splendidly with the dark wood and chrome interior, and the setting sun gleamed off the sleek metal and brought out the warm hues in the wood.

Mark sipped his glass of Talisker whisky and thought of the ring nestled safely in his pocket. Before night, he'd planned to ask for her hand after she'd obtained the Astiri land. He'd grown tired of waiting for Anna to complete this real estate task. He knew some might look down on his decision to make his broker his fiancée. Yet, he'd never been overly concerned with outsiders' views concerning what they might consider crooked ethics. He'd decided he'd propose tonight. Even if she didn't accept, he'd give her time to think it over and come to grips with her age and his advantages.

The sound of heels on wooden stairs caught his attention, and he turned his gaze from the high windows to see his beautiful Anna ascending the stairs to their table. He stood from his seat and opened his arms in greeting.

She seemed to pause a moment, an odd look on her face, but then her expression cleared, and she stepped into his embrace with a joking, "Mark! Long time no see!"

Mark chuckled in response and moved to pull her chair out for her, helping her scoot in once she'd perched. "It might not seem terribly long to you, but my world dulls significantly when I don't have your bright smile to lighten my board rooms! Do you remember when you were still in school as an intern, and you'd accompany me on summer trips with Rand Mining?"

He pushed them off down memory lane, along which they ordered their drinks and dinner. Anna obliged him by listening to him reminisce about her exuberant activities as a youth, occasionally adding her own stories into the mix.

"Oh, the architecture in Tanzania was stunning!" she said. "And oddly reminiscent of what's currently being developed in Scandinavia, although with obvious differences in resources. I just wish their innovations were as highly revered."

Mark waved his hand loftily. "One cannot easily sway a market based on historical preference, only make small changes and ride the wave."

"Even if that preference is rooted in racism and xenophobia?"

Mark stopped for a moment, studying Anna's face closely to see if the question was genuine, but she just blinked curiously back at him with her large, hazel eyes.

"Of course," he hedged slowly. "One must always account for history's previous sins."

Anna simply smiled back and took a small bite of her salmon.

Mark took the offered beat to regain his bearings before they moved on to lighter topics and he forgot the moment. The food was delicious, as he expected, and the company was fine. They moved from the main course to dessert, and Mark started his approach over a delectable creme au caramel and coffee.

"Anna, I've been thinking about you quite a bit recently. You know we've been in each other's lives for some time now, and I feel as though we know each other well because of it ..." Mark paused, putting his hand over Anna's. She seemed confused for a moment, but she didn't pull away, so he continued. "Your family is important to me. I've been friends with your father since we were young men, and I've had the privilege of watching you grow into the elegant woman you are today."

Mark took his hand back and slid the ring box out of his pocket. He opened it to show the jewelry to Anna. She stared at the ring, stunned, silent, and blushing, as he kept speaking.

"I know we haven't developed much of a romantic relationship, but I believe that will come, given time. Anna, we could do wonderful things together, you and I. I find you stunning, and I know that marrying me will hold many advantages for you and Adamos Realty. Anna Adamos, will you consent to become my wife?"

Anna sucked in a stunned breath and seemed to struggle for words for a moment.

"Mark I … Dear Lord, I don't even know what to say to this …."

"I know it seems like a lot, but please consider this proposition from a viewpoint devoid of romantic entanglement for a moment. I know you have no romantic prospects, and a woman of your advancing years needs to start thinking of her soon-to-be family. I can offer you comfort and ease in that stage of your life. Juggling motherhood and your business together will be hard enough. So, allow me to lighten your load. And the connections we could offer one another would open whole new sectors of the business world."

"For pity's sake, *Mark*." Anna's brows furrowed. Her cheeks, once pink with surprise, were flushing red. "Children? I can't even believe you started this discussion at *marriage*, and now you're going on about kids?!"

Mark sat back in his chair. He'd expected a bit of push-back, but this reaction seemed more than he'd planned.

"Holy m—" Anna put her hands over her face, her voice muffled even as she continued speaking. Her hands fell into her lap along with her gaze. "No, Mark, I will not marry you."

"Anna, surely if you just take a moment to consider, you'll see the advantages—"

"*No,* Mark," she looked up from her palms with a glare. "My marriage will not be a business transaction, and I certainly will not bring children into a world where my partner sees me as a means to more capitalist ventures! Put that godforsaken ring away." She started scooting out of her chair, pulling her purse off the back.

"Wait, please," Mark snapped the lid shut on the ring and put the box back in his pocket. Anna stopped what she was doing and turned to look. He opened his mouth, about to say something to walk the conversation back when he was interrupted by his phone ringing. He gave Anna a pleading look. "Please, just wait a moment for me to deal with this call, and we can talk a little more. I'd like to know where I went so wrong."

Whether because of their history or familial friendship, he wasn't sure, but Anna looked at him for a breath before giving a terse nod. She let go of her purse, so it settled back where it was. Mark breathed a sigh of relief and stepped a few feet away from the table before raising his cell phone to his ear.

"Rand."

"Mark!" Tim's voice held an ocean of tension with just one word.

Mark grunted back at him, distracted as he watched Anna sip her coffee.

His CFO continued in a tight voice. "It's about the Wesley Estate. It seems the boy found some way to memorialize his land. He fast-tracked the process, and the government approved his proposal this afternoon."

"What."

Tim continued babbling about possible work-arounds and using their influence in Stardade to dismantle the memorialization process, but Mark stopped listening. Mark had worked with various people to *build* the memorialization laws so they were watertight. He wanted to buy up land in Stardade, but some of it was for personal use, and he didn't want anyone else touching those properties. If he went after the Wesley land as part of the National Park System, he'd put his own assets at risk.

The businessman clenched his jaw tightly and took a few deep breaths through his nose, trying to remember what he'd learned about centering himself from a long-ago ex-girlfriend who'd done yoga religiously. After another minute of listening to Tim ramble in the background while he focused on feeling his lungs expand, he interrupted the man.

"Enough. Obviously, the boy was more clever than we were led to believe. Or he had someone help him. Either way, if we continue to push for his land, it will tip our hand more than is wise. Start looking into other plots with similar dimensions to see if we can't transition the groundwork we've already done rather than scrapping the whole project."

"Of course! I'll call the team and get them started tonight."

"Thank you. I have to go. I am in the middle of an important meeting."

They said their goodbyes and hung up, but Mark gave himself another moment to work past his rage before he rejoined Anna at the table. She'd obviously picked up on his tension, and her brows knit in concern.

"What was that about?"

"The Wesley land." Mark felt his jaw locking up again as his anger simmered, and he worked to keep talking normally. "You've been in communication with that boy for a month now. Have you made any headway?"

Anna's reaction was subtle, but she'd grown up with Mark, and he knew her tells. She only paused a moment before hedging. "On and off, yes."

He heard his knuckles popping as he clenched his right hand into a fist. "And in all of this 'on and off' communication, he never spoke to you about the fact that he was in the process of getting his land memorialized?"

Anna sat back in her chair, pulling her hands into her lap, but she didn't reply. She kept her gaze steady on his face, visibly fighting to keep her shoulders loose. Mark's vision went red with anger, and he stood abruptly, his chair clattering onto its back with his motion. He put his palms on the table and leaned into Anna's face.

"Miss Adamos, may I remind you that we have a contract stipulating your efforts to obtain that land for Rand Mining?" He pushed further into her space and lowered his voice dangerously. "I will have my people *crawling* all over this mess, Anna, and if I find even a hint that you've helped that boy keep his land, I will *obliterate* Adamos Realty. I will make you destitute. And when I am done, you will be *begging* me to take you as a wife because, obviously, that is all you are good for."

He could see Anna's fists clenching in her lap, her forearms trembling with either fear or anger, but her voice was surprisingly steady when she spoke.

"I welcome you to try, Mr. Rand. But I would advise you to clean your own hands before trying to point bloody fingers."

Mark snarled, his mind whirling through the possible implications of her statement, but a voice from the stairwell cut off his reply.

"Mr. Rand?"

Mark straightened and looked over, his gaze landing on a man in a cheap suit. He had a badge on a chain resting against his ugly purple tie, identifying him as some sort of government agent. As they made eye contact, the man started towards him.

"Mark Rand, you are now under arrest for suspicion of espionage against a foreign country."

"What?" Mark's eyes bugged, and he moved to back away but bumped against the table. The man quickly gripped his wrist and twisted it around his back, his other hand producing a zip tie from his pocket.

"I am now going to inform you of your rights. You have the right to remain silent. Anything you say and do can be used against you in the court of law. You have the right to attain legal counsel—"

"What is this?! How dare you! Do you even know who I am?!" Mark started yelling over him, even as the man continued telling him his rights.

With a rough hand on the detainee's shoulder and the other on his opposite arm, the man marched him to the stairs. Mark looked back at Anna as they started down. The last glimpse of her face showed him a determined frown and hazel eyes lit with a burning fire.

Chapter 25

The Crash

TALMADGE LEANED HIS head against the tinted window of the SUV and stared at the yellow and orange landscape as it blurred by the car. Anna had handed him off to a set of burly men two weeks ago, and in that time, they'd moved five times.

The men worked for a company called Aldebaran Security, and they were a study in contrasts. Ajani was over six feet tall, with broad shoulders, close-cropped hair, and a bushy beard. His smile was wide, and his eyes sparkled when he told a joke.

In contrast, Kofi was on the slim side. He looked like he was built out of whipcord and barbed wire, and his personality matched. He was at least a half-foot shorter than his companion, with long dreads studded with gold charms and wraps.

The two told Talmadge they'd worked together for close to a decade, and that they would keep him safe. That was at the first safe house, and they'd moved him the same night. The young man had gone with them easily the first time, trusting their experience. The second time, he'd been annoyed but tried to follow their direction.

The third time it happened, he'd just settled in for bed when Kofi had come into his bedroom.

"Come here," he'd said in his flat voice.

Talmadge had glared from behind his covers, but when Kofi had just stared back, he huffed, pushed the sheets down, and stepped out of bed. Kofi led him to another room on the second floor and stopped him two feet back from the window without turning on any lights. The blinds were down, but the slats were angled flat, offering a striped view out of the window.

"Watch," he said, pointing outside to the street.

Talmadge huffed but watched as a car came to a stop at the corner and idled before turning left out of his view.

"Wow, a car," Talmadge said sarcastically. "I've never seen that before."

"Wait," was Kofi's only reply.

After a few minutes, another car of the same variety did the same thing. Was it the same car? Certainly, it couldn't have been. Unless the driver had gotten turned around?

"They're circling the block trying to figure out the best entry points. Ajani recognized the car from the last house, so they haven't been at it long. We're leaving."

Talmadge felt a chill go up his spine but didn't hesitate to pack his Go Bag and escape to the next house.

After that, the pair started pointing out the patterns to their charge, and as Talmadge's knowledge of the men hunting him grew, he felt as though his skin got thinner. He'd never felt so vulnerable in his life. In your head, it was one thing to know that doing something would lead to people trying to kill you. It was another thing entirely to live it. And the thought that Rand, the man Talmadge had looked up to once upon a time, was the cause of his danger made it all more strange.

Outside the car Talmadge was currently riding in, the yellow and orange landscape gave way to a small copse of trees before breaking down into dry grass and scrubbing. The highway they were on was relatively unpopulated, and the scenery utterly somniferous. Still, the man felt a creep up his spine. Twisting around to look out the other windows and out the back, he spotted a car in front and one behind. Nothing, in particular, made them look like they were together. They were different makes, models, and colors. One was at least a decade older than the other. Still, they were both on the larger side and making Talmadge paranoid.

"Are those cars …?"

"Yes."

"Don't worry, we're keeping an eye on them," Ajani sparkled at him in the rearview mirror.

Kofi harrumphed beside him but didn't say anything.

For the next hour, nothing changed. The landscape stayed hot and dry, the two cars stayed a respectful distance away, and Kofi's arms stayed crossed over his chest, eyes flicking between their hunters.

Well, one thing changed. As Talmadge's anxiety grew and he began fidgeting, Ajani reached over to the radio and flicked on the music. He sang along softly, his voice deep and impressive and just relaxing enough to keep Talmadge from losing it completely.

Finally, the scenery started to change. More trees started popping up, and the ground started to rise in the hills around them. As the land rose on their left, blocking their view, and the road curved around it, Kofi sat up, and Ajani stopped singing. Talmadge felt ice settle in his stomach at the change in his companions.

He focused on the suspicious car in front of them as it slowed just a tad. Ajani slowed to keep the distance even, but Talmadge saw the car behind them creeping closer.

Kofi hissed through his teeth, and Ajani grunted back, resettling his grip on the wheel.

"What's—?"

"Hush."

Slowly, the distance closed between the two cars.

Slowly, the trees and hills grew more frequent.

Slowly, Talmadge felt his grip on sanity loosen.

Eventually, the two cars were each less than five feet from their bumpers. Trees flashed by on either side, and their cage shrank.

Kofi's yell was the only warning. A wordless shout that had Ajani jerking the wheel to the right. Talmadge saw a flash of metal and lights to the left, and the world imploded.

It was like sound grew claws and a vendetta against his eardrums and stomach.

He felt something smash the entire left side of his body, and suddenly they were rolling. His world was a hurricane in a car. He caught glimpses of hands, glass, and cloth, all in an untraceable whirlwind.

When his brain started processing again, they were somehow, mercifully, right-side up. There was an irregular, deafening, bursting noise like someone was taking a hammer to concrete. Only the hammer and stone were both somehow located directly in Talmadge's *ear*.

"Ajani, get the *hell up*." Talmadge heard Kofi say, voice strained.

He heard an answering groan.

There was more bursting. Talmadge tried to lift his hands to cover his ears, but they didn't seem to want to cooperate.

"Talmadge," Kofi barked from in front of him.

The young man forced himself to look up. It took more effort than it normally did. That should be concerning, shouldn't it?

"Can you unbuckle your seatbelt?" Kofi's voice was grounding. He was used to following unsympathetic orders by this point. Talmadge focused on moving his right hand to the buckle at his side. It didn't want to, but he got stern, and it listened. He shakily pressed the button to release his buckle.

The blasting was back. Kofi was half in the back seat, one hand braced on the seat next to Talmadge, the other holding a gun pointing out the rearview window. Talmadge stared, his brain not able to process what he was seeing.

"Talmadge, when I say go, I need you to get out of the car as fast as you can. Open both your door and Ajani's. Can you do that?"

"Fast?" Talmadge couldn't seem to find the words to properly express how unsure of his own ability to control his body he was, but Kofi, normally a man of few words himself, seemed to read it in his monosyllabic reply.

"Fast."

Talmadge swallowed and then nodded. Nodding was a bad idea. Talmadge gave Kofi a thumbs up.

The blasting started again, and Talmadge finally put two and two together that it was gunfire when Kofi shot out the back window twice, gun right beside Talmadge's face. The noise stopped after that, and Kofi barked, "Go."

Talmadge scrambled his way out of the car as fast as he could. It wasn't as fast as he'd like, but he was out of the vehicle with both doors open before anyone shot him, so he'd count it as a win.

Ajani was slumped over the wheel, his face badly cut, and his left arm clearly broken. Talmadge swallowed harshly at the sight of bone poking out of Ajani's forearm.

Kofi was on his knees in his own seat, looking at Talmadge over Ajani's slumped form. "Try to get him upright, but don't step out from behind the car doors."

Talmadge nodded in reply. Nodding was still a bad idea.

He tried to block out the sound of gunfire as he focused on getting Ajani out of the car and on two feet. When he finally had the man standing, he looked up to find Kofi had somehow circled the front of the car to come to stand beside them.

"The car that was in front of us is undamaged. I was able to dispatch the driver before he could engage."

Talmadge stared out of words, hands full and unwilling to nod.

"Help me get Ajani in the back," Kofi continued, his eyes and attention focused on their surroundings.

He led the way to the SUV, and Talmadge very carefully didn't look below the rims of the car.

They had just got Ajani loaded when the back window beside Talmadge's head exploded. He felt something hit the left side of his face. His head turned, and his body kept the momentum. He felt his knees turn to jelly. His ankles gave out. He hit the asphalt.

The sight of red blood bubbling against the sparkly white side of an edge marker kissed him good night.

Chapter 26

The Pie

9 Months Later

JAQ FELT HER smile widen to almost painful levels when she finally heard the door open. She tried to tone it down and play it cool before the newcomer saw, but based on the ache in her cheeks, she didn't think she'd succeeded much by the time Talmadge came into view. However, she couldn't feel too self-conscious after catching sight of his own flushed face and blinding grin.

It had taken months to set up their first official date. The Aldebaran Security Agents (they refused to acknowledge the title bodyguards) who were helping to keep Talmadge safe had originally balked at the idea of him staying in contact with Jaq, and she honestly had no idea how the man had managed to talk them around, but he had. That moment had been the beginning of a trend the young man soon adopted of completely astounding (the admittedly very flappable) Jaqueline Fox when she least expected it. Talmadge had such an unassuming way about him to be so willing to throw himself in the middle of conflicts and then hold his ground was forever surprising. Sometimes she caught herself thinking that he was some sort of inhuman creation or fae creature, to constantly trick her into a sense of security and then astonish her with his boldness.

When Mark Rand had been arrested months ago, the backlash had been almost immediate. The agents had tried to squirrel Talmadge away to safety as fast as they could, but there had still been a close call when he had been traveling between safe houses, and an overeager hitman had tried to use his car as a means of completing his contract. The wreck had been a bad one. Talmadge had been rather badly hurt, but his spirit hadn't flagged, and he'd stuck to his guns. Now, Mr. Rand was behind bars for a multitude of lifetimes, and Talmadge had a rather dashing collection of scars down the left side of his face. He wasn't overly fond of them, but Jaq had quickly told him they made him look piratical. While they were mostly a mass of stitches and swollen skin, the description had kept Talmadge's spirits up, but as they healed, it had become the truth.

Jaq wasn't allowed to be by Talmadge's side for any of his recovery. She hadn't even been told of his wreck until a week after it happened. When they were finally able to get in contact, Talmadge had restricted them to phone calls and text, no video chatting. He'd told her about what he could remember of the crash itself and let her know both Kofi and Ajani were alive and kicking.

"Kofi's mad as a wet cat about it, though. He's keeping both Ajani and me in the same room and refuses to leave the safe house until we're both well again. He almost didn't sleep at all, but Ajani nearly got mad that he wasn't taking care of himself," Talmadge had laughed at the memory and then grown serious. "Also, I thought Kofi was the scary one of the pair. I was wrong. Kofi is scary, so Ajani doesn't have to be. *Never* make that man angry."

Jaq had laughed and listened more and slowly convinced Talmadge to let her see him. She'd been braced for something terrible. When he'd finally turned on his camera, it was better and worse than she had expected. His wounds, cleaned, stitched, and bandaged, looked manageable. But he was swollen and bruised and an entire rainbow of painful colors. When Jaq saw, she had to take a breath. But upon releasing it, she smiled and said, "See? Didn't you miss my stunning face?"

Talmadge smiled with the right side of his face and agreed.

⸻◈⸻

Mark being imprisoned was one of the only reasons Talmadge's agents had been comfortable allowing his and Jaq's date to happen. And even then, they weren't allowed anywhere public. The pair had kept in contact via email, texting, and video chats, and that was the only way they were able to coordinate their long-awaited union. Jaq met with one of the agents yesterday evening, and the pair drove to the safe house Talmadge met her at today. It was a new house in a sparsely filled neighborhood. The floor plan was open, with high ceilings and two floors. She'd spent the night in a strange bed with a bodyguard in the next room and felt decidedly strange about the turns her life had taken. Normally, Jacqueline would balk at the idea of going so far just to meet a guy, but this one seemed worth it.

"Jaq the Giant Slayer!" Talmadge crowed, sweeping her into a tight hug.

"Tally Cat," she returned, laughing as he grimaced.

"Ugh, that one is an immediate no… Thank you for playing. Please try again."

Jaq kept laughing, tugging a bit of hair behind his ear. "Well, what do you expect? I've run out of all the good nicknames already! I'm scraping the bottom of the barrel here!"

"I have faith in your infinite creativity," he replied in a serious voice.

Jaq just put her palm over his right cheek and pushed him out of her embrace, still giggling.

"Well, my creativity will have to wait. I have it on good authority I'm owed a baking lesson."

"Based on the thing you tried to pass off as cake on our first meeting, you're owed more than one."

"Oh, you little—"

"To the kitchen!" Talmadge interrupted, grasping Jaq by her unresisting shoulders and guiding her into the kitchen. It had already been graciously stocked by agents, who had put all their formidable bodyguarding skills to the test by braving the grocery store for the pair.

⚍

"Jaq, you are stunningly beautiful, one of the most intelligent people I have ever met, and one of the best people I know. So please know that I say this with all the kindness I can muster … You can't bake your way out of a paper bag."

"I know!" Jaq wailed, slumping over the counter and covering her head with her arms. "It doesn't seem to matter what I do. Everything I bake turns out horrible."

"Dude, this rhubarb pie is somehow hard. How did you manage to make a pie filling hard?"

They had pulled the pie from the oven a few minutes ago, and Jaq had hoped it would somehow magically get better as it cooled, but her dreams were dashed as the minutes passed in agony. She watched as her filling, which had first resembled a bubbling fruit leather, slowly cooled into something ashy and hard. In the end, it looked more like something one might find most easily at the edge of an active volcano or on the surface of the moon.

"I don't know how it did that. Ask the oven! It has to be possessed or something!"

"Oh, obviously," Talmadge nodded along sagely. "It's not at all that you reduced it for too long on the stovetop and then baked out the remaining liquid. No, the only answer is that the oven of this very modern, new, never-lived-in-house has been possessed by a here-to-for, never seen demon hell-bent on ruining anything you bake."

Jacqueline uncovered her face just long enough to viciously stick her tongue out before burrowing it in her arms again.

"Why do you even put up with me?" she mumbled into her arms. "This was your grandmother's recipe, and I ruined it!"

"Aw, Jaq, don't be like that."

"No, but really." She sat up and through blurry eyes, saw Talmadge look at her, crestfallen. "Ugh, this is stupid. I shouldn't be *crying* just because some pie turned out badly. But I really wanted to impress you somehow. I'm just a moron."

"Jaq, sweetheart." She felt Talmadge pull her into a hug, and she tucked her wet face into his neck. "Seriously, you don't have to do anything else to amaze me. I already know how great you are."

She sniffled, decidedly unladylike, and tried to burrow further into him. He stumbled back with a laugh and pulled her in a bit more snuggly.

"I know I've said it before, but I really wish you'd be nicer to yourself," he whispered into her hair as he gently started to rock them from foot to foot. "You don't have to do anything but be yourself. I'll like you anyway."

"Nuh-uh," she shook her head, rubbing snot and tears into his skin.

"Nuh-uh? Nuh-uh, to what?"

"Nuh-uh, you won't like me."

"Now, why do you think that?"

She huffed and let her hands drop from around his back, leaning her full weight against him. "No one else has liked me without me trying," she confessed.

"Well, they're all stupid," he said without missing a beat. She huffed, and he smiled as he continued. "Besides, we all know I have extremely discerning taste, and you are simply the best."

"Talmadge ..." her teary voice held a hint of playful warning.

"What? Didn't you know that? That you're simply the best?"

"Talmadge Clark, don't you dare start singing."

"Better than all the rest!"

"You let me go, you evil man!"

Talmadge just held her closer, turning their sway into a stumbling dance as he continued caterwauling to a pink-cheeked, laughing Jaq.

Chapter 27

The Garden

PHILLIP FELT LIKE his palms would never be dry again. He tried patting them on his jacket as he and Anna took one of their frequent walks from the house down into his family's garden. Over their months of living together, Anna had fallen in love with the place. Phillip had grown up loving it but watching Anna discover its little treasures had brought about a new appreciation for him. He loved walking any of his land with her because of this. Anna had a way of looking at the world that brought new dimensions of beauty and awe to his perspective. Even now, in the early spring, when new buds were only just starting to peek out, and everything was still mostly mud and bare bark, she seemed to find beauty in nature he wouldn't have noticed without her keen eye.

"You okay?" she asked from beside him, her brow knit.

"Huh?"

"You've been rubbing your stomach," she said, gesturing to where his hands were still rucking up the rough canvas of his jacket. "Is it upset? Should we go back inside?"

"Oh, uh, nah. I don't know why I was doing that," he chuckled lamely. Thankfully, Anna accepted it with only a doubtful look, and they continued their walk.

"It's a nice day out, isn't it?" she asked, gamely trying to keep the conversation going.

"Yeah, I think the daffodils are starting to sprout!"

"Oh, I love daffodils! They always make me so happy!"

"Me too. I always thought they were like the flower equivalent to hearing a baby's laugh."

"Yes!" She stopped and turned to look at him, her eyes large. "Exactly like that! They're like concentrated hope with pollen!"

Phillip laughed and nodded. "Got it in one, Adamos."

"You're my daffodil," she said before twinkling up at him and turning back to continue their walk.

Phillip gulped and followed after her, shoving his wet palms into his pockets in the hopes he could dry them more subtly that way. Only that led to his knuckles bumping the ring box he'd squirreled away, which only seemed to make his problem worse.

Phillip and Anna had been dating for nine months now, and she had moved in to live with him for the last six of those. They'd moved fast, but everything felt real and important in a way that made Phillip feel sure about them.

It hadn't been perfect; they'd had arguments, but they'd all been fair fights. His mom used to say stuff like that. She'd tell all her boys to find partners you could disagree with, and neither of you would lose your head.

When his older brother had his first big relationship, he'd overheard her telling him to remember that any time Matthew and his boyfriend had a problem, it should be them versus the problem, not them versus each other. Phillip thought he and Anna did that pretty well, and when they missed the mark, they never hesitated to apologize.

Phillip felt safe with Anna and hoped he made her feel the same. He felt like he could come to her with any problem, and they'd take it apart together. She'd already helped him with his grief, found him a good counselor to start talking to, and helped him recognize that drinking wasn't the healthiest coping mechanism.

He tried his best to help her in return. A few months ago, Anna confessed that she sometimes got in her own head too much and felt disconnected from her emotions. Phillip had worked with her to find ways to check in with how she was feeling, and he tried to make sure she let herself feel things rather than burying inconvenient emotions for the sake of pragmatism. They were a work in progress, but he wanted to do the work, and he hoped she did, too.

"Phil?"

Phillip was startled, crashing out of his thoughts and back to reality. He realized belatedly that Anna had repeated his name a few times, and it hadn't registered.

"Are you sure you're okay?" she asked real concern in her voice now. "You're looking pale, and if you collapse out here, I'm not strong enough to drag you back to the house."

"What? No, I'm fine, I promise."

Anna just studied his face. "I suppose I could tie a loop around one of your ankles and get the four-wheeler to haul you back," she mused.

"Anna, seriously, I'm fine," he insisted.

She narrowed her eyes but relented with an ominous, "We'll see …."

"You got something planned, Adamos?"

"That's for me to know and you to stumble across, Wesley."

"I'd better watch my footing, then."

"Unless that's what I want you to do. You're like a puppet to my mechanicians," she said in a playful voice.

Phillip just laughed at her antics and held out one of his hands. "Well, if I'm to be a puppet, I may as well enjoy the view. Shall we visit the pond first?"

She accepted his hand with a nod and allowed him to lead her there, pulling his arm around her shoulders and tucking herself close to his side.

They meandered their way to the pond and perched on the bench there, watching the flock of wood hoopoes that nested there flit through the trees. Anna sighed and laid her head against his chest, her body loose and relaxed. Phillip kissed the crown of her head and drew in his courage with a deep breath.

"Do you remember when I first brought you here?"

"I don't think I'll ever forget it," she said with a smile at the memory. "Now I know it was all a ploy to finally kiss me."

Phillip smiled at her teasing but continued. "I hadn't visited it much before then because coming here used to be painful. It would remind me of my family."

Anna drew back and looked at him, her eyes soft with regret. "I wish I could have met them."

"They would have loved you," he agreed. "And the lot of you would have made my life absolute chaos."

"I make your life fun. You like it, don't lie."

"I love it," he took one of her hands and placed it back on his chest. "You make my life better; you make *me* better."

Anna's eyes grew large as she slowly caught on, but she didn't interrupt.

Phillip slid off the bench and pulled the ring box from his pocket as he kneeled in front of the love of his life. "Anna, our path has never been a straight line. Neither of us made the best first impression on each other, and it looked more like we'd each be the other's undoing for a short time. But we've never not been important to each other. And the fact that we've grown past that period of adversity has made me the luckiest man in Stardade *and* Valtross. You make me want to be more than I am, and I'd be honored if you'd give me the privilege of making you, my partner and wife. Anna Adamos, will you marry me?"

By the end of his speech, Anna had tears gathering in her eyes, and she could only nod in reply, her voice completely blocked with emotion. Phillip took the ring out of the box and gently slid it onto Anna's finger.

"This belonged to my mother, you know," he said it conversationally, but Anna stilled under his hands, her tears finally spilling over. "I don't know if it was a family heirloom or not. I'd never been interested in that while they were alive. But I like the idea of it."

Anna stared down at the ring. It was a thin band of silver, cresting in an oval cut gemstone of a strange light blue. Two diamonds were nestled at its side, but Anna couldn't get over the stone's color.

Phil seemed to read her mind and explained, "I had it appraised, and the man said it's real. It's a blue topaz."

"It's the same color as your eyes," she said, glancing between the ring and his face to make sure. "How?"

Phil laughed, caught her hand, and kissed the back of it.

"Oh my God, you're the worst," Anna whispered, her voice choked.

"Sorry?"

"I was going to propose to *you*," she explained, pulling another ring box out of her jacket pockets and popping it open to show a silver band nestled in the blue velvet. "I had everything planned out perfectly, but then you beat me to the punch and did it so much better than I ever could. You're the worst!"

Phillip threw his head back and laughed, absolutely smitten with Anna's frustration. "Wait, no," he said, his voice still full of mirth. "No, I still want you to do it. Show me. I want to see!"

Anna swiped at her tears, "But I can't, not after that. You did so good! How can I follow *that* whole speech?"

"Come on! Please?" He took the ring box from her hands, closed it, and shoved it back in her pocket for her. "Here, we'll reset. We'll pretend like I didn't just make the best proposal ever, and you can surprise me this time!"

"Ugh, no! Yours was so good it made me cry, and now my makeup is all messed up. I can't propose to you with runny mascara!"

"Anna, sweet angel of my eye, brightest moon pie, sugar gumdrop princess Anna, *please* propose to me?" Phillip blinked up at her with the widest eyes he could manage, and she finally caved to his begging.

"Fine," she groaned. "But only because I love you!"

Phillip grinned in triumph and climbed back up to sit on the bench next to her.

"Where should we start?"

"Give me a minute to get my head straight," she insisted before grabbing his arm and pulling it back around her shoulders.

They went back to watching the birds for a time, and Phillip felt them both relax back into the moment. Finally, Anna stirred under his arm.

"You taught me about trogons. Do you remember that?" she started, turning to look up at him. "We'd been hiking in the woods, and you got super excited because they're apparently super rare."

He nodded, smiling at the memory and in anticipation of her teasing him for his bird-watching.

"Who knew I'd fall in love with some old man excited when he spots a new bird?" she ribbed, and he wrinkled his nose at her. Her smile softened as she got back on track. "But you taught me that they're a monogamous bird. The males dance for the females, showing off their bright colors in the hopes of catching her eye and keeping her forever ..." she trailed off in thought for a moment, still watching the birds, and Phillip let her be, eager to see where she was going.

"The first time we met, I was stunned by how blue your eyes were." She turned to look at him, studying his eyes with intensity. "Your colors caught me," she whispered, "but what I saw as I got to know you keeps me. You're so strong, Phillip. You form connections with everyone around you, and you raise everyone up. You can be selfless to a fault, and your gentleness and thoughtfulness make me so proud to call you my companion."

Phillip felt his face heating, and a lump started to form in his throat. Anna stood from the bench to kneel in front of him and pulled the box from her pocket to show him.

"Every morning, I'm blessed to wake up beside you, and every night I thank all my lucky stars for everything that led me to you. Phillip, I love you so much, and I know no one else will catch my eye. Will you marry me?"

Phillip blinked rapidly, trying to keep the prickling in his eyes from turning into real tears. He tried to keep his voice even as he replied, "Only if you do a mating dance for me."

Anna blinked in surprise before laughing and shoving him on the shoulder.

"You're a buttface, Phillip Wesley. I take it back; I don't want to marry you!"

"No takesy backsies!" he cried, yanking the ring box out of her hands and quickly fumbling the ring onto his finger. "See? I'm yours now. You can't give me up!"

Anna laughed as she clamored back to her feet and dropped herself onto his lap. "Don't think you hid your tears from me, either. I saw your eyes watering."

"Nope, you lie. There was no such thing."

"Was so. I totally got to you," she insisted, tucking herself into his chest as he leaned back to make room.

"All right, you got me," he agreed. "It seems I'm so in love with my fiancée that I cry when she proposes to me."

"Fiancée …"

"Seems like it. We've got these rings and everything to prove it."

Anna fiddled with her ring for a moment in silence. Phillip was about to ask if she was all right when she sat up from his chest.

"Phil," she said, voice small and gaze still locked on her ring.

"Yeah, baby, what is it?"

"Um, you want to have kids, right? Like, we've talked about it, and you don't want your family name to die with you, so you want to have kids."

"I mean, not right away, but yeah, I'd like to have a kid or two."

Anna's brow scrunched, and she struggled for a moment before continuing. "You know I'm already over thirty, right? I know you want kids, and I want them too, but I also want to grow my business, and I just don't know how to make it all fit …."

"Anna," Phillip reached for her face, but she had her eyes shut tight, not willing to look at anything. "Sweetheart, I want kids, but I want you to be happy more than anything. We can wait as long as you need before we try … But I think you also forget that I can pass on the Wesley name to any kid willing to call me his dad. We can find a kid to adopt and bring them into our family or get a surrogate. There are so many options, and while we don't have all the time in the world, we certainly have enough for you to relax a little and help me find what works the best for us."

Anna's eyes flew wide, and she gasped in a little breath, looking at Phillip a little lost and a lot in awe.

"I love you, sweetheart," he whispered. "We'll find something for us."

"I love you, too," she said, winding her arms around his back and burying herself in a hug. "I love you so, *so* much."

Chapter 28

The Ceremony

THE ADAMOS SIBLINGS, their mother, and Jaq readied themselves for the ceremony in the bride's quarters. Jaq, the maid of honor, looked stunning in a carnation-pink sheath dress that matched that of Abigail, Anna's younger sister. Adam, her older brother, wore a white tuxedo and pink bowtie to accent the girls' dresses. Talmadge, Phil's best man, was downstairs wearing the same tux.

Though Talmadge's security agents had argued that he should avoid the wedding, he had insisted the intimate event's secrecy would provide enough security. Not to mention, there were half a dozen bodyguards, one for each guest, hired by the Adamos family. The guards were stationed outside the home, ensuring everyone's safety. The wedding party had done their best to keep this high-profile wedding private.

Anna sat down in her reading chair, which someone had pulled to sit in front of the dresser mirror. Examining her reflection, she checked her teeth for lipstick. She wore her long hair in stylized curls with braids from her temples tucked under her veil at the back of her head.

Her chipmunk cheeks were rosy from both makeup and nerves. She fiddled with her engagement ring in her champagne-colored princess dress strewn with red and pink live roses.

This large room and its adjoining bathroom made up the top floor, and private hosts' suite, of the Crossed Stars Bed and Breakfast. When she and Phil had established this business together, they had seen promising results throughout the first year. In retrospect, Anna wondered if they weren't insane for planning a wedding during the inception of a business.

However, the business partners had manifested the success of every one of their endeavors. Upon the anniversary of their small business, they met with the older owners of the Starlight Inn. The Stellas were Phil's only neighbors and competitors. Putting on her best broker's smile, Anna proposed that the Stellas sell their inn to the younger couple. Without even a counteroffer, the older women accepted the proposition, excited to retire after years of trying to scrape together enough money to do so. Once Anna handled the paperwork, the Starlight Inn became a satellite location for Crossed Stars, exponentially increasing the partners' revenue as they scaled up their business. All the while, Adamos Realty prospered under the excellent management of her younger sister and eager protégé.

Anna was proud of the small inn locations they had founded within their home and the valley. The Wesley house provided the perfect locale, with the best view on the island, for hikers interested in staying inside the national park. Close enough to the historic district to enjoy its amenities, people traveled from all over the world to visit the five-star hotel and its secondary location. The cherry on top of the patrons' visits were the private tours conducted by the man who grew up running around these lands, the park ranger himself, Phillip Wesley. Anna used her international influence to market this incredible experience, which she had the pleasure of living every day of her life. On this day, she would solidify the rest of her life in this dream come true.

Though they had thrown around the idea of getting married in the family garden, they loved keeping the place a secret for explorers to discover. Because the Wesley Memorial Park was national, public property, anyone could happen upon this garden while on a hike. However, when Anna asked Phil if this fact upset him, he explained that this possibility best honored the memory of his family. After all, the legacy of this land for its people was what they had worked to protect for their entire lives, up to and including their sacrifices.

Huh, my feet literally feel cold, Anna realized with a giggle as she lifted her wedding dress to look at her champagne ballet slippers. She wiggled her numb toes. *Must be from how fast my heart is pumping.* She touched her chest, feeling the organ's rhythm that belonged to the man downstairs.

Her mother, dressed in a navy-blue pantsuit, fussed with her veil, saying, "Are you sure you don't want an updo?"

"Yes, Mother," she sighed, "I'm certain."

"I still don't know why you'd prefer living in the middle of nowhere to the amenities of Prijipati."

Anna sighed.

She suspected this sentiment was born of her mother's nerves. After all, today marked the first of her children's marriages. She reflected on the countless heated discussions she'd had with her mother about her decision to move to another country to live with a "lower class" man. Her mother was appalled when she told her parents about her intentions to marry him. She had finally found the key to a tentative truce when she explained her upcoming nuptials like a business venture. She loathed to internally thank Mark for that tactic, but it had worked. She was already in business with Mr. Wesley, so their marriage made smart business sense. And what she and Phil shared couldn't be contained by simple concepts like a government contract.

"Mom, leave her *be*," Abigail chimed in. "The ceremony is in ten minutes."

"Mrs. Adamos," Jaq said, working to gain her attention with excited gestures, "can I get you anything?"

"Here." Adam handed Anna and their mother flutes of Champagne. He then passed a glass to Abigail, then Jaq, and held up his own glass. "To Anna and her bright future."

"To Anna," they sang.

"To Anna," Dad said as he opened the bedroom door, ready to go in his white tux with a navy-blue bowtie. "Are you ready, tiger?"

She nodded, feeling her eyes mist as she took in the image of her family and good friend supporting her on this journey to Stardade. This marriage was a symbol of their families coming together in love. Jaq handed the bride her bouquet of dusky pink roses and purple lilacs, the fresh flowers' divine aroma enveloping her.

As Abigail, Adam, and Jaq made their way downstairs one at a time, Anna took her father's arm. To the sound of the hired violinist playing the wedding march, they ventured down the staircase. She admired how the rose-and-lilac decorated banister accented her bouquet. The sunlight from the floor-to-ceiling windows warmed her skin. The photographer and the videographer captured every moment, which she knew would be lovely to watch for years to come. At that moment, though, she could only focus on the man at the altar once she saw him.

As she descended, her gown floating around her, she saw her groom looking debonair in his black tuxedo. With the backdrop of the mountains, valley, and ocean, he looked like a prince from her childhood fantasies, standing within the walls of his elegant castle. Both of the betrothed started crying tears of utter joy when their eyes met. His awed expression, blurred by her tears, was worth more than his weight in cobalt.

Once at the altar, Anna's father kissed her on the cheek and stood with the others, facing the couple. Behind Stardade Judge Williams starting the ceremony, rain pitter-pattered against the windows and down over the vista. A mist rose up from the valley but soon evaporated as the intense sunlight shined despite the rain.

"Look at that," the judge said in her soft voice as everyone paused to observe. "Mother Nature both rains and shines on this blessed day."

The beautiful ceremony proceeded without incident. The betrothed recited the traditional vows of each of their home countries.

"Before God and these witnesses, I, Anna Adamos, take you, Phillip Wesley, to be my lawfully wedded spouse, to have and to cherish from this day forward, for the best, for the worst, whether wealthy or impoverished, in illness and in wellness, to love and to adore, until death leads us together beyond."

"Before Mother Nature, I, Phillip Wesley, take you, Anna Adamos, to be my eternal companion, to have and to embrace from now forevermore, no matter what may come, no matter our wealth or health, to love and to appreciate, to admire and to adore, from now on into the afterlife."

Upon the ceremony's completion, the judge announced, "You may now kiss one another."

Phillip placed a hand on her cheek as she leaned in for the much-awaited kiss. Her heart galloped like a freed racehorse through the valley. Their intimate yet modest kiss set her body aflame. Tossing her bouquet off to the side, she wrapped her arms around him. Later, she'd discover Jaq, all smiles, had caught the bouquet.

Their intimate reception included fine Stardadian cuisine of stew shared around the Wesley dinner table. Of course, Anna insisted on ringing the bell at the start of the reception. The hearty meal, not unlike one from home, impressed even her Valtrossian family. Everyone adored the strawberry cake, which they had hired a bakery to make rather than take a chance on Jaq's baking skills.

As tensions unwound and the crew loosened up to enjoy one another's company. The new spouses settled into their shared family. The small group shared dances, stories, toasts, and jokes late into the evening. Surrounded by their loved ones, Anna couldn't imagine a more perfect beginning to the future she had only dreamed possible before she came to Stardade.

5 Years Later

ANNA LOOKED UP from her book when she heard the tea kettle whistle in the kitchen. She lounged in her favorite armchair in their living room, cozy in the sunlight streaming through the windows. Outside she beheld the splendid view that had captivated her since the first time she'd witnessed it. She caught the swoop of a hawk as the bird flew over the protected valley. In the twilight, the raptor flew towards the ocean. The waves crashed majestically against the beach in the distance.

Phil entered the room bearing a tea tray with a piping hot kettle and cups. The pair had found the set buried in a cupboard at the Starlight Inn and tried to return it to the Stellas, but the ladies had insisted they keep it.

"It was a wedding gift from her parents," Elena said, holding her wife's hand. "It's blessed our marriage for more than fifty years, and now it's time it blessed someone else."

"Besides," Lucia chimed in. "Elena bought a fancy new device that takes up the whole counter and can make a worse cup of tea, so why would she want to hang on to that old thing?"

"Oh fooey, don't listen to her. She's just fussing to fuss. You two keep it, and may it bring you both happiness."

The tea set had, indeed, brought them happiness. It had become a tradition for the pair to drink a cup every evening as they watched the sunset together.

Anna set down her book and started to get up to help, but Phil caught her before she could get far, saying, "I don't think so, Mrs. Adamos Wesley. You know I am the designated tea courier of this household."

She felt her cheeks heat at her husband's tender use of her married name. He kept the traditions of their household so regular that she could set her watch to them.

"Oh, before I forget," she said. "Did Jaq and Tal RSVP for our first party meeting?"

"You know, I thought once all was said and done, you'd be too tired of subterfuge to start up a rebel Unimona Party faction."

"Me, tire? Never. Are they coming?"

"Of course, but remember your promise to me."

"No rebellions until we form a unified, trustworthy circle," she recited in a flat tone. "It's just a brainstorming session."

"Mhm." He narrowed his eyes and raised his eyebrows as he walked towards the coffee table. "Let's hope brainstorm lightning strikes."

She set down *Wuthering Heights* on the end table next to the framed picture of the two Wesley brothers in the garden with their fish. Not for the first time, she admired the Celtic knots Phil had wood burned into the frame he'd crafted for the treasured memory.

"Remind me," she said as he set the strong-scented chamomile tea on the coffee table to pour them each a cup, "who caught the fish in this picture?" She pointed.

"Well, when Matthew told the story," he said, mixing the tea with honey and lemon, "he always swore I would've lost the fish if he wasn't there to grab it with the net." He blew on the beverage for his wife. "But I technically reeled in that monster."

"Ah." She shook her head fondly as she took her cup. "That's why I can never recall."

"It's still very hot, my love."

"You know I'm always careful, Mr. Protective Pants."

"With a name like Mr. Protective Pants, I don't know why you didn't just take my last name."

"Har, har!" she said with sarcasm. "You forgot I *did* take your last name."

"As a hyphenate."

"It's not a *hyphenate*—Will I never hear the end of this?"

They shared a hearty laugh.

"Truth be told, I don't care a wit," Phil said, sitting down with his own tea. "I just like to bug you. You get all feisty, and your cheeks get all red and cute."

"You certainly keep me on my toes." She sipped her tea, which was all the more delicious when made with such care.

"Is it too hot?"

She rolled her eyes in response.

"I'm glad we can be ourselves around one another. No matter if our last names are different."

"So funny," she said with a teasing tone. "What's in a name?"

"Who said that again? Brontë was it?" he asked, pointing to the novel next to her. He sipped his tea.

"For a second, you almost had me going there." She giggled. "I know your favorite is Shakespeare."

"That which we call a rose, by any other name, would smell as sweet," he quoted.

"I love when you wax poetic."

"I love you, my wife." He stood and leaned over her chair to plant a tender kiss on her lips.

"And I love you."

The sunset through the window, casting the pair in molten light as they leaned together, basking in the radiant glow of day's end and each other's love.

Thank you for reading
Crossed Stars

Your opinion matters. Let us
know what you think.

Review this book on your favorite
book site, review site, blog or
your own social media sites
and share your opinion
with other readers!